NOT INVITED
TO THE
WEDDING

A Forward Forever Romance

Mimi Laurence

Mimi Laurence
Visit my website at
https://mimilaurencewrites.wixsite.com/words

Printed in the United States of America

Publisher: Janice Seto

ISBN-13 978-1-926935-44-7 (ebook)
ISBN-13 978-1-926935-43-0 (print)

DEDICATION

To the real Paul and Elayne Henderson

Mrs. Ada Johnston

And to the
ORIGINAL
Kathy Brantley

Your act of kindness inspires us all.

CONTENTS

ACKNOWLEGEMENTS

To my publisher, Janice Seto, this book would not be published without her.

CHAPTER ONE

Bin here

EARLY SUNDAY MORNING IN LONDON, WHEN THE SUN mistily opens up its eyes after a cool wintry Saturday, is hardly silent. A few stragglers slurring their lament at the sun's presence mingle with city workers sweeping up litter and washing down the unfortunate rejection of the last round at the pubs. Bleary-eyed people slurp their lukewarm coffees while shuffling through the staff door for their morning shift at St. Hedwig's.

Professor Baron Marc Thoe van der Veer stood to one side of the old-fashioned door, not an automated type that swished back, but one that only swung out. Against some clause in the modern building and fire safety code, the door was number 311 on the list for repairs so the staff just put up with it.

Despite his own tiredness, the senior consultant nevertheless allowed the incoming pedestrian traffic to delay his leave-taking. It had been a worrisome few hours but his tiny patient pulled through and now was safely in the hands of the regular medical team, many of whom numbered among the incoming staff. At last, after 4 minutes of courtesy, he made his way out the door himself, yawning hugely, and rubbing his eyes. Which is why he did not spot a nurse, halfway along the driveway, standing still with her eyes closed, directly in his path.

When an immovable object meets irresistible force, physicists have told innumerable science students, the outcome should be annihilation. In this case, the curvaceous staff nurse, not at all an immovable object, gave way to his 18-stone frame. She fell all the way down to the concrete pavement, but was saved from an inglorious impact on her bottom by the Professor's long steadying arm.

"Not in any hurry to go home, Staff Nurse Smith?" he asked silkily, "You are standing outside blocking everyone's way because...?"

In a peevish mood, forgetting that esteemed professors should be addressed with a high degree of respect, the mousy-haired nurse responded with a snap, "I certainly am in a hurry to go home for my days off, sir, I just worked a double shift because of nursing shortages. Another last-minute added shift, the third this month."

Taken aback by her spirited diatribe, the Professor made suitable amends, "My humble apologies, Staff Nurse, you are very tired..."

"What I am tired of, sir, is the never-ending nursing shortage. That Brexit vote made it worse..."

she slapped her palm over her mouth. "Sorry, sir, we are not supposed to speak anything about politics."

"No need to apologize, you are asleep on your feet. It is not surprising that your eyes are slammed shut. Let me drive you home."

She looked up mussily at the Professor. This was not the first time the blond giant gave her a lift back to her basement flat. He had the most beautiful Rolls Royce, he has the most beautiful manners. Although his manner towards her had cooled somewhat since those enchanted weeks last fall: museums, theatre, and dining out snatched between shifts. It was nothing she could pin it on, as he remained professional as always. Still, she could sense that something had changed since November. Maybe he sensed she was dangerously close to falling in love with him while he saw her only as a pleasant companion...

"Oh, that is not why I have my eyes closed. I don't want to see that." She pointed out to the outer edge of the old hospital building as they crossed to the medical staff parking area. Abutting St. Hedwig's is the Church of England outpost in this salubrious area of the East End. Worn, darkened by decades of London smog, and hours of cars and buses puffing out various chemicals from their tailpipes; it stood anchored in a distant past, forbidding.

"You are of the atheist persuasion?" the professor frowned as he was the latest of a long line of staunch Dutch Calvinists.

"No, of course not..." she broke off, "Oh, now you've done it... I can't un-see it..." she wailed, and ran off, hurtling to the side of the church, then falling onto her knees, around the bins.

In full pursuit, the Professor had time to extract a large snowy white handkerchief from his immaculately tailored suit. This would not be the first time he would mop up someone from St. Hedwig's being sick. A double shift would tax anyone's immune system.

Reaching the crouching too-thin staff nurse, the Professor offered his handkerchief for her usage.

"Thank you, sir, this is just perfect."

A minute later, while he averted his eyes, Katharine rose to her feet, slightly unsteady, clasping his handkerchief to her ample bosom. Forlornly, she muttered, "I really, really tried not to see you... but I can't help it."

The Professor knew he could put down her emotional utterance to fatigue and ignore it. But he could also speak frankly and provide answers to her unspoken questions. The American parlance summed it up as giving her closure, with the truth, clichéd as it was "It is not you, it's me."

"Katharine..." he began.

She looked down mournfully into his handkerchief, "What am I going to do with you? I am squeezed for money as it is..."

"Kathy...?" he inquired, questioningly. Katharine, unfortunately, did not hear the nickname Marc had taken upon himself for his exclusive use in the fall. After all these months of wintry formality, she would have been gladdened by his involuntary utterance.

Tucked in the middle of his handkerchief was something fuzzy and black: a little bundle of fur, mewing pathetically.

"I thought I saw something dodging cars and scrounging for food in front of the church, sir. Up close, I see why, his poor eyes are matted together. He couldn't really see where he was going..." Katharine's eyes filled up. "So, what do we do now?"

He decided, right there and then, to discard his preconceived limiting notion regarding women, that 'if it ain't Dutch, it ain't much'. These months of avoiding Kathy were all for nought. Only one brief conversation, in this unlikely place, put paid to his valiant efforts to avoid what he now knows is the inevitable.

This was an unexpected opportunity to make up for it all. The Professor decided then and there to twist Fate to his own advantage. As he propelled Katharine and the tiny all-black kitten towards his car, he smoothly intoned, "I will call this vet I know and have this creature looked at immediately."

His eyes crinkled at its corners, "Since I have the vet at hand, Kathy, the only outstanding issue is his name. What would you like to name our little creature?"

CHAPTER TWO

Say My Name

THE STRANGEST THINGS COME IN HANDY, thought Katharine, sitting inside the Professor's warm car, carefully holding a carton of milk to the lips of the dirty little kitten. The milk was still warm as yet another rest-break had been interrupted by another RTA before Katharine could open her drink. The kitten was slurping it with pathetic speed as the Rolls Royce raced out of the East End. Trees began lining the streets as the smarter parts of the capitol opened a well-bred eye.

As the Rolls Royce purred to a halt beside an imposing Regency house in Little Venice, Katharine looked dubiously around her. "Your vet lives here?"

"She is meeting us here," noted the Professor as he had stepped out to open the door at her side. Both standing before a door that was polished to an inch of its life, the Professor extracted a key, but someone by magic opened it from inside.

A comfortable body, Mrs. Drew greeted them with a stern, "There you are, sir, late for your breakfast, and Doctor Gibbs in the morning-room here is just finishing a cup of tea."

The Professor opened a door to the left of the hallway where a thin bespectacled woman in her 40s was looking through the Sunday papers in the stately room overlooking the river, "Good morning, Marc, what have you for me this fine morning?"

"This is Staff Nurse Smith, from St. Hedwig's A&E department. She found this little thing... let's proceed to my clinic... Katharine, this is Dr. Doris Gibbs."

"How do you do, Dr. Gibbs," offered Katharine as the little party worked its way past family portraits in a wood-paneled hallway to an austere, functional examining room. She offered the matty, filthy little beast to the all-of-a-sudden motherly vet. Prompted by the vet, she related how the little kitten came into her care.

Handling the tired little beast with gingerly care, Dr. Gibbs muttered as she poked and prodded. "...8 ounces... barely passed newborn, about a month old."

"So young to be all alone," choked Katharine.

The Professor placed an arm around Katharine, while Dr. Gibbs tried not to look too speculative at her friend of long standing, "He's not anymore."

Katharine sucked in a breath. This is not the first time she had stood so close to the Professor but it was the same every time, a frisson of awareness. Breathe in, she told herself, must not get distracted. So much is at stake, think of your goals, the rates, the bills... Focus. You have no time to spare. Stop these foolish thoughts. He must never know.

Dr. Gibbs gave them a shooing motion, "Go with Mrs. Drew or the porridge will go cold. Let me and the kitten be."

The conservatory was set out with crisp linen and a place setting for two in the desultory first Sunday in March. It had been too long since Katharine enjoyed such a feast at breakfast. The atmosphere was convivial, talking about tastes in literature, Greek philosophy, baroque music...

"I suppose he needs scrambled eggs, crispy bacon, smoked salmon, Italian peppers, porridge, beans, and homemade jam just to fill up that vast frame," she thought, as she thanked Mrs. Drew for the fluffy scrambled eggs before her. Katharine glanced at the Professor, contemplating on how well he filled out his suit, how happy life would be waking to mornings such as this... Unexpectedly, the Professor caught her gaze, raised a wry brow, which was followed by a slow smile. Katharine pinkened, and stared back down at her plate, as if the solution to the Rosetta Stone was embedded in the Royal Doulton...

She babbled, "I should be going... it's Sunday... church... going to visit my mother later..."

The Professor responded coolly, "All in good time, we should wait for Dr. Gibbs."

In no time at all, the vet pronounced the kitten ready to go to a good home. "Poor thing is suffering from a minor eye infection – this medication will deal with that in short order. The new forever-home would have to deliver medication into the infected eye several times a day. I even de-wormed it," she said smugly, "I am prepared for all sorts of surprises. And later on, the follow-up will be more feline vaccines."

Drew, the Professor's butler, hoovered at the clinic door with an old cat basket and an old soft baby-blue blanket. This charitable act served another purpose, as Mrs. Drew had earlier hissed at her husband, "Take Jasper's basket and see for yourself... she's a real lady. After that last one, he might finally see the sense of a good wife and provide us with a proper mistress of the house."

Smiling at Drew, Katharine said, "So thoughtful of you, Drew. And could you please thank Mrs. Drew for the delicious breakfast. After a frightful night at A&E, I am grateful for a meal."

The Professor scooped up the kitten, which licked at his wrist, and gently deposited it inside the basket. The dear kitten snuggled into the blanket with the gratitude of one who had rarely known kindness.

Turning to Dr. Gibbs, Katharine began, "I would like to give my contact information to settle the account later for the kitten..."

"Think nothing of it, Miss Smith, my husband and I have a wonderful arrangement with Marc." She brandished a bag of medication and cat food from her case like a teacher pulling out a stack of graded papers... "Feed him milk like a baby three times a day and eye drops four times a day."

The sun was beaming lunch greetings as the Professor navigated his automobile through the streets of London with his precious cargo. "You shall be seeing the world with fresh eyes soon," murmured Katharine, leaning over the back seat.

"You will have a new home and we shall look after you."
Privately, Kathy quailed inside at the higher grocery bills with
a hungry kitten... she sighed, thinking it was high time she
shed a few pounds.

The Rolls Royce pulled up to a once-glamorous terrace
house in a formerly posh street in the East End, sliding to a
halt beside Katharine's basement flat. It was handy for St.
Hedwig's: it was close to the buses, and most important, it
was free of mortgage. Before he died, Katharine's brother had
signed over the deed to his younger sister.

Opening the car door for Katharine, the Professor reached
for the cat's basket, the bag, and the box with assorted items
for the little kitten's comfort. "No, I insist in carrying this in
for you. You cannot possibly manage everything."

As they reached the basement door, it was flung open with
a flourish. "Oh, Professor, good morning, you brought
Katharine home again! Good of you," smiled the man built
like a rugby player.

He nodded his bright red head at the Professor, and
grabbed the box, "There you are, Katharine, what an
atrocious overtime. I boiled a couple of eggs for you and even
got more of your favourite yoghurt. The water is hot in the
shower, all ready for you, and then... bed."

"Kevin, how sweet of you to think of my breakfast..."
Katharine smiled her thanks at his thoughtfulness.

"Staff Nurse Dickenson, good morning to you," intoned
the Professor, looking down his splendid nose on the
grinning ginger-haired Kevin Dickenson. "Thankfully the

eggs will keep. Miss Smith has already had breakfast... a full English breakfast."

Katharine smiled shyly at the Professor, "I shall always associate scrambled eggs with smoked salmon, thank you."

"The most important meal of the day, cutting corners is not advised," accepted the Professor, casting a derisive eye at the egg cups and yoghurt tub set on the kitchen counter.

Oblivious to the comparison of meals and other undertones, Kevin galumphed over to the cat basket set on an elderly table, "Now what have we got inside this basket? Hey, there," he peered at the kitten, "Let me guess, Katharine, we have an addition to the family?"

The Professor winced at this laddish humour.

Barely awakened from his nap, the kitten was sleepily affronted as Kevin gently and determinedly extracted him from the basket and deposited him onto the floor with more enthusiasm than sensitivity. The tiny thing stumbled cautiously on the IKEA rug, looking curiously and warily around him, desperately seeking the familiarity of mousey locks or fair hair.

"Well, what shall we call him?" wondered Katharine as she knelt and gently stroked his black fur -- soothing the kitten.

The Professor was pensive. "It has been my experience that cats know their own name..."

"How does Shadey sound?" Kevin got onto his haunches, and beckoned with his bulbous fingers, "C'mon over, Shadey...!"

An immediate loud hiss at Kevin from the little scrap of black fur surprised everyone in the room, the kitten's ears outraged at the prospect of being summoned by that name henceforth.

Looking at Katharine's worried face, the Professor got onto his haunches. Studying the bundle of injured pride for what seemed like half an hour, Marc waited for the kitten to lock eyes with him. Softly, he spread his hands wide and asked, "Would you be 'Coenraad'?"

Transfixed, the kitten looked unblinkingly at the Professor and ambled over into his right hand, purring lowly. As the Professor stood up, the kitten rubbed his furry head into the well-tailored suit, sighing contently. Katharine looked round eyed at Marc.

Slightly smug, the Professor intoned, "I do believe our kitten has made his choice, Kathy."

CHAPTER THREE

A House by any other name

"MAMA, I HAVE BEEN FOOLISH," Katharine apologized, springing up from the Brit-Rail stop at Warminster, thrusting the cat basket into her parent's arms. "His name is Coenraad."

Her mother --sensibly clad in a cardigan, tweeds, and Burberry-- nonchalantly took hold of the basket and steered her only daughter to the awaiting vehicle. "Oh, what is he like?"

"Pathetically starved and living in the streets."

Eyes widened, but valiantly keeping a straight face, "Do tell, dear, how did you meet?" as she placed the cat basket in the back, giving the sleeping baby cat a stroke through the mesh.

After tossing her bag into the boot, Katharine got into the driver's seat, "Meet who?"

"This Coenraad you are foolish about...?"

"Oh, Mama! That's the name Marc gave my new kitten. It is foolish of me to take in a mouth to feed," as Katharine steered through the country roads at dusk. "At least I do not have to worry about vet bills and the medication for Coenraad's eye."

"Oh, really, that's a comfort... Marc again?" her mother probed.

"Well, yes, this morning his vet did an examination at his house..."

By the time the Mini turned into the drive for home, Katharine had been expertly wrung dry from the morning's events: the breakfast, and the length of her acquaintance with the Professor. "Wonder why he is helpful all of a sudden..." mused Katharine's mother.

Katharine pretended that parking at the cottage took all her attention. Indeed, she had by force of habit driven up to the porch of Smith Hall, the Grade II-listed country house looming grandly over the darkening fields and hills, only to realize her mistake and turned back down the drive to the cottage, "Sorry, Mama, I forgot."

"I feel the same..." Mother and daughter were lost in their thoughts, remembering the happy times, before the accident that slowly and inevitably deprived them of the three men of the family – the matron of her husband instantly and her father-in-law weeks later, and then her only son; the daughter of her father and grandfather and finally, her dear brother.

In the past year, since the innumerable operations and rehabilitation stays, the final sad months of palliative care, then totaling up the collective death duties, each monthly visit home fell into the same pattern. Boarding a train at Waterloo station, her mother meeting the train, and then going home. As always a lentil vegetable soup sat burbling away on the Aga. "Who needs meat at every meal?" her mother would lightheartedly dismiss. Over soup so thick that the spoon could stand on end, dinner conversations started with hopeful chats about prospective buyers; a review on the too-low offers.

The majority of time, they had poured over bills and ways to economize, in the cozy sitting room. Whatever could be given up was indeed given up – the animals, the television, the subscription to the theatre and ballet and museums, the vehicles except for the Mini – determinedly cheerful. It had hurt immensely when they had to close the stables, though she was thankful her faithful mare is still in the neighbourhood.

Katharine had taken on all available overtime at St. Hedwig's, derived pleasure from each discounted produce she could find at the local store, and swore off makeup. Her mother had found other jobs for the now-surplus household staff of the big house. Their faithful housekeeper Mrs. Dean tearfully went to the vicar's, and her mother herself moved into the dower house, and took on a part-time secretarial job at the church that was created especially for her, although everyone made it look like it was nothing of the sort.

Each month, their collective efforts saw the rates, the utilities, and the insurance for three properties, all duly paid for. When only when Smith Hall is sold can most of the proceeds be used to pay the death duties.

Smith Hall could not be left empty, the insurance company insisted, and Katharine's mother with a rotating crew of villagers had to be on-site during the day. Although a chore, at least the Queen Anne-style house with its imposing portico, rambling gardens, and arable parkland held a beauty of its own.

The entire neighbourhood rallied around, taking turns as volunteer crews gardening and mowing the grounds of Smith Hall with the former lady of the house. As Mr. Betts, the verger, stated in his booming voice, "Must keep the estate grounds looking right for the best price."

It could not go on forever with Katharine getting thinner and thinner and her mother more lined with worry. "Mama, maybe we are being over sentimental," queried Katharine hesitantly during Christmas. "We had hoped to sell the big house and retain ownership of this dower house. But for months, we have not received any serious offers under those terms. Maybe with the new year, we try a new approach? If we agree to sell everything lock, stock, and barrow, more than likely, we will get more offers. We would be able to settle the death duties and all our bills. And be done with it."

Katharine had gazed at the ornamental Christmas tree tucked inside the fireplace, continuing in a small voice, "You could move into the flat..."

Her mother had looked at her daughter with misty eyes, "Darling, I have been thinking too. We both hate big cities. I can move in with your Aunt Emma. We both can move in with Aunt Emma."

A darling snug house, where many a happy family vacation was spent with the widowed Aunt Emma. It was three stories tall and sited in the countryside near a small village.

"I have come to the same conclusion about the dower house. We are ready to let it go. And we start fresh. How clever of you to have done the Erasmus program during your nursing training."

Katharine rushed over to hug her mother, tears in her eyes "Mama, being together is a splendid idea." She grasped her handkerchief, thinking that never seeing Marc again striding through the halls of St. Hedwig's, even hearing the cool formality of `Staff Nurse Smith` was something to mourn.

Shaking the dower house, March was roaring out ahead of spring, with the kitten yowling almost as loudly as more of the loathed medication was dropped into his eye. Little Coenraad was only placated by his new grandmother feeding him tenderly with a bottle full of warmed nutrient food. He suddenly became a tiny snoring thing snuggled in a soft woolly basket by the Aga, blissfully unaware of yet one more eye treatment to come later that night.

Katharine said the grace and they spooned up their dinner, glad of each other's company. In the weeks since New Year's, their topic over dinner had always started with discussing the sole offer for the entire estate. Afterwards, in the chilly sitting room, the two women looked over the correspondence, too many bills, and the annual notice of an astounding increase in rates and insurance starting in May.

Amidst the gloom was the previous week's letter from their solicitor bidding them come to his office on Monday, the next day, "I will be so grateful when this is all said and done -- not to have rates and insurance for the big house, this cottage, and my basement flat. Once this purchase takes place, 'the happiest couple in Britain' can deal with all that."

"Not much longer now," murmured her mother, stroking the kitten in his box. "Ten o'clock tomorrow, we shall be holding a cheque."

At the offices of the solicitors, Daniels & Gilbank, Katharine and her mother, in their finest clothes which had seen better days, presented themselves promptly at 10 o'clock Monday morning. "As it was a rare treat to have a lie-in," Katharine had thought, looking at the ceiling from her single bed as she waited for her mother to vacate the bathroom, "I shan't get up till 9." It's so quiet in the countryside, no buses rumbling, and no sounds from the empty paddocks. Then she heard her mother padding downstairs to prepare breakfast, and with that, reluctantly scrambled into her slippers.

While waiting, Mrs. Jones, the cozy receptionist who guarded the legal team with the ferocity of a lioness, greeted them as longstanding clients. "I see that Miss Jane is on the cover of another Hello!" she flourished the color magazine, "they have nicknamed her 'Our Princess Jane' already."

Katharine that very minute regretted leaving on her bedside table the library book on William the Silent. She wanly accepted the magazine, because she had been brought up well, which was helpfully opened at the photo-spread, with her cousin, the Honorable Jane Smith-Brantley.

"Anticipating moving in after the honeymoon?" murmured Katharine's mother, peering over her shoulder at the late twenties strawberry blonde with her Prince John, "of 'the Happiest Couple', they even called her 'the new gardening chatelaine' at Smith Hall."

Katharine replied with a sniff, as the family solicitor came out to greet them.

Old Mr. Daniels seated himself slowly after seeing to his clients on the other side of the old-fashioned partner's desk. "My dear ladies, there is yet another delay to the final sale..."

"Oh! What now? We are not getting the cheque for the first half...?"

"Your cousin has made reference to the boiler and the garden..."

Katharine's mother made a well-bred snort, "Nothing wrong with the boiler. Which is not what I could say about my engaged niece and her fiancé..."

"Apparently the gardens are not in quite the condition they had seen it earlier... As for the farmland for organic planting..."

"It is March and they saw it at the New Year. Of course much needs to be done in the spring..."

"Regardless, it is their position that the estate now worth less because of the failure on your part to upkeep and maintain the grounds. They counter-offered with a new purchase contract stipulating a 10% reduction in the purchase price as compensation. Also, they have decided not to issue a cheque for the first half and have defined a new purchase date to two months from now, right on the day of their wedding."

A gasp echoed through the wall paneled office, followed by a spirit of gloom. Katharine mentally quailed at the amount of overtime she would need to do for the bills for two more months. "Stuff and nonsense," snorted Katharine, "This is the third delay they want since January. And now May..."

Her mother raised a handkerchief tremulously to her eyes, "Surely there is no need for these types of tactics? Like his elder brothers, Prince Johnny has inherited quite a generous sum from their mother... Please excuse us for a moment," her mother begged.

Mr. Daniels left, giving them ten minutes, upon which Katharine and her mother tearfully held each other. This would drag on, yet again. However, there was an end goal in sight; the "Hello!" spread indicated that.

Getting straight to the point with Mr. Daniels, Katharine sighed, "We have to dance to their tune, don't we? They are serious about Smith Hall, they gave us the only offer, and they are just playing these silly games. When exactly is the wedding date, Mr. Daniels?"

At his raised brow, her mother said, airily, "It seems to be the trend for brides to not invite her own family to her royal wedding."

On the drive home, Katharine sighed, "Until the wedding, we cannot afford to lose focus, Mama; we are asset rich but cash poor, so I will need all my wits to take on all the overtime for the next couple of months."

Her mother patted her arm, "And I too. Let us pray for stamina..."

"Let's also pray for a miracle..."

CHAPTER FOUR

Foreign Aid

THE PROFESSOR WAS IN A MOOD, a very pensive mood, his Registrar noticed, spending the cloudless April morning keeping a respectful distance. She and the other members of his paediatric team and medical students girded themselves for the imminent day's march. At the rear, the hospital staff, ruled by the iron-hand of middle-aged Sister Donna Yaro, assorted nurses including two foreign nurses, Leslie from Winnipeg and Peta from somewhere in Eastern Europe; the social worker, the physiotherapist, hopped from tiny bed to tiny bed in the ward, as Marc appeared well pleased by each child's progress. Mentally, he was reviewing the bidding; Operation 'Dispatching Dickenson' was on track.

He was well-satisfied with how he sent up Dickenson a few weeks ago: better food, better with animals and better company for Kathy. Looking at the grinning giant in nurse uniform at the tail end of his ward visit as he dismissed the paediatric team, Marc resolutely kept a cool disinterested look on his face as everyone filed out. All the little patients screamed with delight at the antics of Staff Nurse Dickenson, who joked around as he tended to their needs. Marc silently sniffed dismissal; amateur comedians can make a girl laugh but humor fades quickly. In his summation, Dickenson had become some sort of habit for Kathy. Well, habits can be replaced.

Kathy had been most grateful for his offer of a lift to Waterloo station, while he regretted not been able to take her and the kitten to her mother's home. "Mama would have liked to meet you...."

Of course, what mother would not want to meet this eligible bachelor?

Unwilling to be falsely modest, the Professor wore the mantle of his profession as well as he did his suits from Saville Row. In these modern days, even his checkered personal history was not held against him by ambitious mothers and daughters who "hustle". Those in the know were all too aware that the Thoe van der Veer family had enjoyed wealth and property since the Dutch Golden Age. Equity in blue-chip companies, steady dividends, and rents in the present day funded a lifestyle that was as well-to-do as discreet. Law, research, and medical professions kept them out of the media. Their overseas portfolio includes a house in London, villas in the Mediterranean and Portugal, a cottage in Scotland, and other family properties in Europe and the Americas.

All would have been his as the eldest son, had it not been for his youthful rebellious first marriage. Achieving the milestone of medical school graduate and a foothold onto his Fellowship, the 24-year-old Marc had chafed at invisible family expectations and struck out on his own, daring them to voice their true opinions about his new set of friends, his new pastimes, his unconventional intended bride...

Still pensive, the Professor turned a corner to exit the building and Staff Nurse Katharine Smith slammed right into his waistcoat. Marc reached out an arm to steady her, looking disheveled and fatigued. "Oh, sorry, sir, this is getting to be a habit!" Katharine turned beet-red in embarrassment.

"Working extra shifts at A&E?"

Her pallor had returned, "Yes, that too. Off in one minute. Haven't been sleeping much..."

"I sleep very well but I get my daily kitten scratches," Kevin added, good naturedly, as he passed them by, returning to the paediatric ward, "I give Conraddy a poke in the eye last thing at night or first thing in the morning and he puts up a fight, he does. Easier for me to do the drops, as I can't do all the extra shifts."

Marc stopped himself in time from reprimanding Kevin, swallowing what he wanted to voice *"When you are smug that your woman works herself to the bone to keep you, there's something unmanly about you."*

Instead, Marc smiled down at Katharine, "To make amends for crashing into you, allow me invite you to lunch. You can tell me how our kitten is seeing the world..."

She brightened, looking up at him with a spark in her eyes, "Oh, I would love to, his eyes are clearing and he is getting plump..." then she recollected, forlornly "Dear me, no, I can't, I have another night shift tonight."

He pressed on, "But you would like to..."

"More than anything..." she caught herself, from throwing herself into his arms and howling about her troubles, and instead mumbled, "More than anything, I have to get home and, uh, get to sleep..."

Katharine sighed in relief, at not blurting her entire story. When she was tired, it was hard to keep her feelings under tight discipline. Satisfied with his morning's work, Marc took her arm without further question and led her out to the consultants parking area.

Opening the door to the flat, Katharine saw an upended fern plant entwined with black fur. "Another one," she sighed. Coenraad unabashedly greeted Marc like a long lost friend. The professor could see that in the month since living with Kathy and Kevin, the black kitten had turned from a pathetic scrawny wee scrap into a little tear-away. At the sight of the eye dropper, Coenraad mewed plaintively and burrowed for escape in the crook of the Professor's sleeve. Marc nonchalantly inserted the drops in little Coenraad's eyes. A mulish kitten, he nevertheless took his medicine like a man.

"Well, I suppose he allows you license as a paediatrician," murmured Katharine. "He digs his claws into Kevin somehow fiercely."

Marc gave a murmur, "We all have different tastes..." taking Coenraad as an ally.

The phone rang, Katharine leaped to her feet to answer it. It was from Daniels & Gilbank, "Yes, this is she. Oh, Miss Gilbank... you have Mother there too? Please don't tell me another hitch, I cannot bear it..." Over her shoulder, she saw Marc get to his feet, "Please hold on..."

Without having to ask, Marc offered, "This sounds important... Would you like me to go and give you privacy?"

At her nod, Marc concluded, "If this turns out to be a matter of gravity, I want your word to share with me."

Tapping the mute button, Katharine nodded, with her fingers crossed behind her back. The Professor stepped closer, gently took the arm with the guilty fingers, deposited the slumbering Coenraad into her palm, and closed the door behind him, a gleam in his eye.

Miss Ada Gilbank, the younger daughter of the elder Mr. Daniels's partner, cleared her throat, "In light of unsatisfactory progress of contractual fulfillment on the part of the Honorable Jane Smith-Brantley and His Royal Highness, might I suggest you and your mother consider a new offer that just came in. It is from a foreign buyer.

"I understand both you ladies felt it important that Smith Hall stay in the family. The entail does stipulate that Brantley House goes to the male heir, in this case, your uncle who has taken possession. However, your London basement flat and Smith Hall and its park and farms were not included in the entail, so you can do with it what you wish. The late Lord Hampton deeded Smith Hall to you both. Its situation abutting the Brantley House estate property makes it practical for your cousin and her fiancé, but you are not bound by their preferences."

Like dew struck by sunlight, Katharine's sleepiness abated, "Please tell me more about this surprising offer...."

It was a fair offer. Although the sale would conclude with a later purchase date, the end of August, the new closing date was compensated by matching the original offer price of the Jane and her royal fiancé, 'Farmer John'. Although Katharine was a bit sad that Smith-Brantley's living on the Smith estate would end after six centuries, she was rather done with the unnecessary meanness of the past few months.

All of this was subject to a satisfactory inspection of the house and the grounds. The call ended with a promise to email the offer-to-purchase documents and the deadline of a fortnight away for their response. The handsome sum as non-refundable deposit upon agreement made her gasp. Cousin Jane and Prince Johnny`s deposit of 1,000 pounds paled in comparison. Katharine sighed in relief. Just on the deposit alone, she could settle the death duties and need work no more overtime.

An hour later, her mother's relief was clear over the phone, "How auspicious, Katharine. Our prayers are answered. We have several pages to review. Compared to your cousin, this is 'bird in hand worth two in the bush'."

"Just four more months of rates and insurance and bills..." exclaimed her mother happily, "Finally, the best prospect of this load off our shoulders, you can stop working yourself to a thread."

"Hurry up and wait," thought Katharine, tiredly dreading a few more months of waiting, as she patted a nourishing serum on her wan face. Freshly showered, she was asleep within five minutes with Coenraad curled up on the small scatter rug by her bed.

CHAPTER FIVE

Cheque, please

WEEKENDS IN THE HOME COUNTIES, ON THE ESTATES of friends, were all well and good, however, in the end, there is nothing like a home of one's own. Lady Hampton had gathered a cabal of other mothers in relating the latest plans for the upcoming royal wedding, while her noble husband held forth in the billiards room. "There are plenty of country houses on the market with farmland..." wheedled her daughter, the Honorable Jane Smith-Brantley, into the ear of Prince Johnny of Wales, as they sat in intense conversation in the drawing room of Brantley House, "We don't need Smith Hall."

But the Prince remained stubbornly unconvinced, "It is the land. I had my heart set on Smith Hall because of the land. It is just right for organic farming and raising livestock, we would have a sustainable agricultural model farm."

He shifted a bit uncomfortably, "As a consequence, my father has offered up that house again as a place for us to live."

Jane frowned. She had balked at the offer of a cottage on the royal estate before, and her resistance to a lease from her future in-laws has not shifted one iota. The eyes of his family and Royal Household staff would hoover over their every move. That was not for her.

Since their engagement, Jane and Johnny had spent months discreetly looking at suitable country homes to purchase and make their base and always, grudgingly, they had come back to Smith Hall. It was quietly situated, unlike the home of one brother who lived directly under the flight path to Heathrow airport. Very little renovation needed, as the late Lord Hampton's father had poured much capital to modernize the historic building. In the heart of rural England, Smith Hall suited Jane, a country woman at heart. "I don't want to live under the kindness of your family."

The Prince patted Jane's shoulder, "Neither do I. We overplayed our hand on Smith Hall, the best thing to do is match that new foreign offer they have and throw in a sweetener or two."

"They will ask for more," she warned, "And this wedding is costing enough."

He laughed, "I am going to be the envy of my brothers, with a wife who scrutinizes the household books with a fine tooth comb." As the band brought the music to a close, he drew her close and Johnny whispered, "It is far enough, away from London, that even at full price, it is a bargain. There is enough left over that we can also afford that villa in France."

"I beg your pardon for shouting, Miss Daniels, but why exactly do my cousin and Prince Johnny have any say in this other offer?" hissed Katharine into her mobile phone. Thankfully her mobile phone has rung while she was in the linen closet on a frightfully busy Monday. "They have the nerve ask for us to deal with them still, by matching the foreign offer?"

The tenacious solicitor murmured, "The purchasing contract with your cousin and the prince does give them the right to put forth a competing bid that matches or exceeds any other offer you are considering before the date of final sale. It does you no harm to consider it. I shall email you the offer."

With one hand on her mobile phone and one hand counting the linens, Katharine's eyes darted from shelf to cell phone. She opened up the attachment and her eyes popped wide at the new amount offered.

"They could have had Smith Hall cheaper if they had not engaged in tomfoolery," grumbled Katharine in silence, feeling reckless. She read it over more carefully later on over her tea break while the other staff nurses scanned the paper. Juliana, the Toronto nurse from women's medical, groaned, "The pound has fallen against the Euro again, I am so glad I paid for my share of Lolita's hen-do already. Ibiza won't be so affordable now."

That gave Katharine an idea. She could hardly wait to call her mother and the solicitor.

It was 4 days later in the staff loo of the A&E department that Katharine could check her mobile phone, which has vibrated not three minutes earlier. At last, confirmation by the bank that a cheque for a satisfyingly large amount of down payment had been deposited into the separate accounts of Katharine and her mother came in. The solicitors can use that to settle their bills and duties and taxes. Her mother texted a confirmation in the midst of packing and labeling boxes of personal possessions and family mementos for shipping to her sister Emma.

She was almost weeping with relief, and fatigue. Another 16 hours shift with nary a break for the loo. After making her report to the ward supervisor, and advising personnel that she was not taking on any more overtime, Katharine unhesitatingly bolted out of the door. It was a bright afternoon, sunlight breaking through even the grimy neighbourhood of St. Hedwig's. As Katharine walked tiredly, it was with mild pleasure towards the church.

Passing the bins, she thought it was barely six weeks since baby kitten Coenraad came into her small world. He likes a clean slate, clearing the mantelpiece, the dinette set, and coffee table of obstacles such as vases, plates, and cutlery. After the inevitable scolding, the kitten feigning innocence curled into the chest of Kevin who was slumbering on the sofa -- two males snoring after a fashion.

Katharine found her usual pew with a creak as she swung the door open. Releasing the brakes over her emotions, she got down onto her knees, resting on the pew in front of her, and buried her head in her forearms. Four years, three burials, two years of overtime, and, now the peace of finality. She was grateful.

Now that the debts were all but settled and no more future bills related to Smith Hall; she was unfettered. In the immediate short-term, no more overtime, she gave herself a watery smile. And more time in the bath. As for her future...

Katharine was contemplating the stained glass windows in the cool dark church. How nice to sit and not rush off to bed or a shift or to shop; the treadmill has stopped and she has had enough of that. Now she has the world at her feet. A degree in nursing, on the state register, time on the Erasmus program, a facility in languages, she can go anywhere in Europe, the world was her oyster. If she wanted to shake the dust of the East End off her feet, she could move in with Aunt Emma and her mother, her beloved mother, now that there were no grandparents, no father, no brother; it was just herself and her mother.

On the other hand, she could stay in a fully-paid up basement flat in London. Despite the impending Brexit, it was still London, close to Zone 1, close to the theatre, concerts, museums... and close to the man who also loved them, Professor Marc Thoe van der Veer.

The old vicar was escorting a couple completing marriage lessons out the door. He came up the aisle and smiled at Katharine. "Ah, Staff Nurse," as she was still in uniform, "do sit awhile."

"Yes, sir," Katharine bowed her head in respect, "I merely come for refreshments, 'Come all ye who labour and are heavy-laden...' "

"...and I will refresh you,' – yes, Matthew 11:28. I find you much in good spirits, is there something you would like to talk about?" asked the vicar as he sat in the pew in front and turned around.

"The clouds have parted somewhat, and now I see before me a fork in the road."

"Prayer helps to discern which path you choose. Is it the one that leads you closer to your highest self?"

"Both do. Nurse here in London or Nurse if I move with my Mother. Either place, I shall nurse."

"Why would you stay here?"

"Um," Katharine flushed a bit pink...

"A gentleman friend?"

"Very much a gentleman..."

"Why would you leave?"

"My Mother. The family I have left. Brexit."

The old vicar paused, "Do not rush to an answer, let it come to you, perhaps it will come in your dreams," He gave her a reassuring smile, as the verger beckoned him, "Rest and pray, child."

Katharine sat in a reverie that was half daydream and half fatigue...

"We seem to meet in the most unlikely places, Kathy," intoned the Professor. Startled, Katharine gave him a nod, as he joined her kneeling, "I hope you don't mind. Some respite in the day. This is what the trendy call 'meditation', is it not?"

"What a coincidence that you are here too."

"I contrive to make the most of good fortune. I saw you as I drove in for a short round," He nonchalantly disclosed. "How is the kitten seeing the world?"

Eagerly she regaled him about the latest Coenraad adventures, "He has found life worth living and is intent on living it to the full. Now that he is free of eye medication, the kitten has a mission to rid the flat of ferns and plants, in whatever form...."

"My good Mrs. Drew has a cat like that too. I wish I were in one place long enough to have a dog again."

Katharine murmured sympathetically, "Mmm, you have one foot in two countries... how do you feel about that?" she ventured.

"Is it like that trendy term of 'microswitching'? You are betwixt and between, 50-50 -- Unanchored."

"Uncommitted... some would say," Katharine offered. "Until you make a decision, which one is your real home, the 51%, you are rootless and dogless."

"If what you say has weight, Kathy, then London is where I have my house..."

"A darling location... how long have you had it?" she smiled at remembered flavours of the lovely breakfast.

"My godmother left it to me shortly before I married. It is my only home; my late wife would have preferred a flat in South Kensington."

Katharine was startled at the thought of so many meals and outings she had with Marc, not knowing his exact marital status! "I thought you were a bachelor, not a widower. And I thought you lived in the Netherlands?"

"I was born and raised in the Netherlands. The rest of my family live there. When I visit or lecture or see patients, I do stay with various family members. But I have no other home than London."

Katharine heard confirmation that London was his home. Not his main home, his only home. She made up her mind, I would put up with almost anything to be near him. Turning in the pew, she fixed her gaze at him, "London is my home too now that my mother is moving in with my aunt."

He smiled at her words and took her hand, "It has been a while since I took you out for dinner. The day after tomorrow, I have tickets to the theatre, but dinner first. I will call for you at 6 PM." The Professor was smug as his Kathy no longer talked or even thought about Dickenson.

CHAPTER SIX

Key Workers unite

THE NEW PURCHASE AGREEMENT was quietly negotiated under the radar due to the incessant coverage of the upcoming wedding ceremony, reception, honeymoon, clothes, and flowers. Prince Johnny, a bit more sangfroid about the whirlwind of activities, shrugged, and advised his solicitors and bank to deal with it. Deep into the current issue of Country Life, he was already anticipating the pleasures of farming his own fields. The baby of the family, born years after his brothers, he was out of the spotlight in agricultural college and his gap years on working ranches and farms in Canada. After they married, he and Jane would carry out any royal duties around their interest in rural issues.

It was a tedious shift ending the month of May - a two-week stretch of non-stop emergencies including head injuries sicking up, and little girls attached to tubes and bandages yowling pathetically for their mamas. Katharine scooped up her bag and made her way out of the A&E, her mobile phone back in her pocket. Drat the short-staffing, she fumed, I shall have to dash now to catch the next train home.

Just about to depart from the hospital himself, the Professor saw Katharine dart out the side door. Moving surprisingly fast for someone of his size, Marc caught up with her at the intersection.

"Going somewhere?" He asked chattily.

"Just home, sir, and then a train to Mummy for the weekend."

"What a coincidence, I am just heading in the direction. I can run you home."

The next thing she knew, Marc had bundled her into his Rolls Royce and they headed towards her flat. "I have everything in my shoulder bag, no need to go to the flat."

"Coenraad the kitten..." he reminded her.

"Oh, he is fine with..."

"Oh, he would prefer to be with you."

Katharine knew that to be true and was thankful.

Parked before the steps past the tubs of colourful plants which she had put out to bring some colour to the brown dull neighbourhood; Katharine turned to Marc, "I will just be a minute..."

"Surely that is so as I will help you with your bags while you shower and change out of your uniform."

Katharine looked down at her uniformed self, she did need a cleanup.

The shower was just turning off as Marc and Katharine closed the front door. She called, "Please say there is enough hot water left!"

"You got it right!" a strong cockney accent responded. Within seconds, the door was thrown open and Staff Nurse Paul Henderson walked out, clad hastily in a track suit.

Marc`s eyebrows shot high, wondering if Kathy was one of those kinds who needed any number of men dangling on her arm.

Paul was calling over his shoulder at Katharine, "Lots of the hot... I just had a quick one..." He noticed Marc, "`Hello there, Professor, so you staying here tonight? I just changed the sheets so you can just crawl in."

In the dimness of the basement, Marc`s look of outrage did not register with the other occupants in the flat.

Paul pounded on a bedroom door, "Hey, Kev, we`re running late for the next shift... I`m coming in for my uniform."

Dashing into the bathroom, Katharine murmured over her shoulder to Marc, "I won`t be too long."

Marc, having decided to take advantage of the situation, replied, `Take your time, I can run Henderson and Dickenson to St. Hedwig`s."

Inside the Rolls Royce, Marc made the most of the drive to the hospital, asking searching questions of both staff nurses without seeming to pry. "Prof, you a good friend to her, for those rides. She deserves it," stretched Paul, enjoying the entire back seat to himself

"She keeps to herself, we know she`s got lots of bills to pay..."

Paul sobered, "We all do. We take as many overtime shifts as possible, which is easy due to the nursing vacancies that are yet to be filled here. If it weren`t for Katharine, no way we could do them and go home on the BritRail."

"FailRail, I call it...!" Kevin sniffed.

"Too expensive and too chancy. Katharine`s flat is around the corner from the hospital, so to speak, and I can do about 3 overtimes a week and spend a couple days at home with my Elayne, Mrs. H."

"Now, we don`t take her for granted, Katharine got these second-hand beds for our room and don`t charge for anything. But each night, I put 5 pounds in the jar for the water and gas, she won`t take anything more. Kevin Junior`s school fees are eye-watering..."

"Giving her cat a jab in the eye and cleaning the bath and knicking some loo paper from the hospital..." At the professor`s raised eyebrow, Paul amended, "I mean, loo paper from the pub, we do that."

"And we tell off pesky delinquents trying to hang about."

In less than half an hour, the Professor had dropped off the staff nurses, procured a large cup of hot tea from a shop, and popped in Katharine and the cat basket. "You are a dear, Professor, I needed to get away and missed my tea," murmured Katharine, taking hold of the steaming takeout cup of tea he had offered her.

Po faced, Marc steered his way through the teeming London street, "I had no idea Dickenson was your tenant..."

Katharine looked in askance at Marc. What was the senior consultant from St. Hedwig's sounding so cool about? And looking so smug?

She looked down at the slightly-shabby leather gloves on her lap. "He`s not..." At his searching glance, Katharine started again, "Strictly speaking, he`s not. None of them are."

"There are more...?" He was learning more and more about Kathy every minute.

"There is an ordinance of sorts against short-term rentals. Something to do with housing shortage and AirBnB. So I cannot run afoul of that. Please keep this to yourself." She looked beseechingly at Marc, "You on the medical side know we have mandatory overtime but most of the nursing staff cannot live in London, even East End London. Since they took away the nurses' homes as part of hospitals, the knock-on effect is we nurse have to rent where we can find a place. And where can we key workers afford anything in London within even Zone 6, let alone Zone 1?

"And how can we safely practice if we are beyond exhaustion with overwork, overtime, and long travel times? Leslie and Felicidad occasionally stay in my room. Kevin and Paul have families and they share the old storage room we converted. Kevin is my most regular, you can say." She gave Marc a baleful look, "I do not soak my friends for rent. Their contributions help us all get by."

Marc looked thoughtful, "I wish I had known about this, I would have offered..."

Katharine looked at him with some pride, "I know you would have, but we manage. There are many others of greater need of assistance. But thank you."

"Now tell me how to get to your Mother's home... And why you are beset with all these bills."

"On the condition that you just listen. Three years ago, Grandfather and father and my brother Edward were driving back home from London one night when their car was hit by a drunk driver. Father died instantly, Grandfather a few weeks later. My brother was seriously injured," she stopped, gathered herself, "Many operations, much time in rehabilitation, and private hospitals. Not that we do not like the National Health but we had to act fast for Edward."

She sighed, "And then suddenly, Edward died. Now we have to deal with the death duties from him too. Mama and I are close to settling all our obligations. We now have a good price to sell our home, a firm deal at last."

He smiled, "You are resourceful in ways I had no knowledge, Kathy. If you are not proud of your efforts, let me tell you that you should be."

"Thank you, Mummy and I are glad this is almost behind us. We expect the rest to be behind us very soon."

His eyes intent on the road, Marc inquired, "Does that mean if, I beg your pardon, I mean, when I ask you out that you would have more free time to accept..."

She looked down at her gloves again, "In all likelihood, perhaps yes."

By unspoken mutual agreement, they turned to their common tastes in French opera and chamber music.

Katharine and Edward had often delighted in their grandfather taking them to Covent Garden, the immediacy of live performance.

All too soon, as directed by Katharine, Marc drove through the open gates to Smith Hall estate and up to the dower house, where Kathy's mother came out with a smile. "My daughter texted me that she got a lift home from the hospital. How do you do, I am Katharine's mother, Mrs. Smith-Brantley."

The Professor impressed Mrs. Smith-Brantley with his manners, "Marc Thoe van der Veer, how do you do? The pleasure is mine, Mrs. Smith-Brantley."

Marc glanced at Katherine who was pretending a great interest in Coenraad's basket, as they were all ushered into the dower house, "I wonder what other delightful secrets you are harboring, Staff Nurse Smith. Why are you simply 'Smith' at St. Hedwig's?"

She mumbled, "It is easier to fill out a form as Smith than Smith-Brantley..." Katharine looked up awkwardly, "Oh, I suppose you do know all about it, being Thoe van der Veer."

"Yes, it is a mouthful, and sometimes it is easier for others to just say Van der Veer. Because it is inaccurate, I cannot let it go at that. Of course they say my name in full at Leiden University Medical Centre."

Mrs. Smith-Brantley gave a start, "The Leids Universitair Medisch Centrum?"

"You speak Dutch, Mrs. Smith-Brantley?"

"As does my daughter."

Marc asked Kathy, "My dear Staff Nurse Smith, did you not think that you come from a family of Hollanders would not interest me?"

Katharine fired back, "We are not Hollanders at all; we are Frisian."

They all laughed as Mrs. Smith-Brantley invited the Professor to join them for a light supper. "So you are the Marc who is so helpful with our dear little kitten," Katharine groaned inwardly, her mother was a dog with a bone.

Seated in the kitchen with little Coenraad snug on his chair by the Aga, Katharine realized there were two people who could be dogs with a bone as Marc returned to the subject at hand, "If I had known you could speak my language, Kathy, I would have curbed my language at the hospital."

"You did turn the sky blue on occasion. Several in fact, and I pretended not to know."

"So, why?"

"Well, I did not want to butter you up. Many people probably do. And that is not me. And later on, I just did not know how to say it so I just... let it drop. It was a silly thing to do."

Over a salad and a ham omelet washed down by fresh apple juice, Mrs. Smith-Brantley extolled the excellence of her daughter, to her extreme embarrassment and to the Professor's secret delight. "Do not say you are silly, my clever girl. Marc, a competing offer for the house brought my cousin and fiancé back to the table. Willing to pay the full original amount; there will be nothing like talking us down any more. We asked for outrageous items."

"Mummy and I had originally wanted to retain the dower... so we proposed they pay the original full amount plus allow us to still keep this dower house."

"This is a dower house for what house?"

"The Smith Hall, up the hill. Easy enough for them to split this dower house from the estate." Taking a sip of tea, Katharine felt slightly wild, "And we learnt from our previous mistake, we asked for quite a good faith deposit down payment of 200,000 pounds, non-refundable...! Within 48 hours. That settled our death duties and bills and rates."

"And this was the icing on the cake; Katharine asked that the balance be paid in Euro at the exchange rate of two days before the Brexit referendum!"

"Euro? Very clever of you, Kathy, to factor in the exchange. Why is that important?"

She raised her chin, "You know how the economy is doing..."

He examined her closely, "Why not the American dollar? The Swiss Franc? They also hold their value vis-à-vis the British pound."

Katharine bluntly stated, "Brexit from the EU, anytime soon..."

Her mother could see the way the wind was blowing, "I am moving home to live with my sister. British pounds are no use in Europe. Marc, maybe you can persuade Katharine dear to leave the bright lights of London for Friesland."

As Katharine was hoping for the ground to swallow her up, Marc answered, looking straight at her mousy locks, "Or maybe there are other reasons for her to continue to work at St. Hedwig's and make her home in London."

CHAPTER SEVEN

Lost in the Royal Mail

"THERE IS A FAMOUS POP SONG, `WORKING FOR THE WEEKEND`, that sounds like what you are about, walks and all,` Feli mentioned archly, as she and Katharine were preparing for bed.

"I do like my job, but it does get to be a bit much. "

Feli was unabashedly up front that she was only at St. Hedwig's until her two years were up, and could be a quality candidate for a hospital job back up north. Cheaper to rent and save up to buy a house, she was well on her way, thanks to Katharine.

Katharine herself had a timeline of another 6 months. To keep burnout at bay, she would give St. Hedwig's and Marc until Christmas. In that time, she would know if Marc would be husband material. To date, they were indeed `working for the weekend` or stolen moments for a walk or coffee or a concert.

Katharine refused all optional overtime shifts and was sleeping much better, even with a roommate gently snoring on the next divan. She closed her eyes too, next morning Marc was taking her to the RHS Chelsea Flower Show. The previous week, when she had been talking about planting some flowers near the dower house's kitchen garden, he offered an outing to the flower show for some ideas. Life in an East End basement flat seemed very colourful now that she had excursions with Marc to look forward to.

Katharine was adjusting her wide-brimmed straw hat just so after returning from Morning Prayer when the dark grey Rolls Royce purred to a halt at the flat. She quietly bolted up the stairs to the pavement where the neighbourhood curtains were twitching. Marc held the door open; his bristly-chin grazed her cheek as a greeting. She remarked in concern, "You look like you were called out all night at the hospital..."

"Not all night, just a couple hours, and the patient is recovering in the ward."

"Dear me, let's cancel. I should let you catch up on your sleep..."

"Oh, a hearty breakfast looking at you in that pink dress over scrambled eggs, a stroll around the flowers, and a lunch together will do me more good!"

Mrs. Drew had before them scrambled eggs with rosemary sprigs, thickly-cut bacon, and grilled tomatoes at an instant. Smiling her thanks at Mrs. Drew, Katharine returned to something that had puzzled her, "Doesn't the flower show open to the public starting on Thursday?"

"Oh, it does, but we are welcome today. Courtesy of former patients of mine, a couple affiliated with the royal Horticultural Society and others are with Royal Hospital Chelsea."

Katharine gathered these were veterans or something like that later on as she and a clean-shaven Marc made their leisurely way around the booths and the garden displays under a vast canopy. Here and there, sunlight trickled through, leaving the ornamental trees, bushes, and flowers preening in their dress rehearsal for the upper class crowd expected later in the week. Bliss, she thought, arm-in-arm with Marc, lingering at what took her interest, backtracking as they chose.

Unlike the regular ticketholders paying upwards of 107 pounds each and relentlessly albeit politely ushered one-way through the display path without any possibility of lingering or walking back to a previous display. How lucky I am to be here with all the time in the world, undisturbed by crowds. One could be miles in the countryside...

"Please look this way, Ma'am!"

Katharine and Marc had turned a corner and happened upon a busy photo shoot in progress. A middle-aged balding photographer, in a three-piece summer suit, dapper, with a rose in his lapel, was directing half a dozen young women silhouetted against a traditional English garden backdrop. Lighting technicians, makeup artists, wardrobe people, staff of a society bible... all encircling the Honorable Jane Smith-Brantley.

She was speaking into her mobile phone, on the verge of tears, "I am glad you are getting patched up, Clarissa dear, but is there the slightest chance you can get here soon?"

A general murmur passed through the assembly. "We have only another 90 minutes here and then we have to pack it in..." the photographer's chief assistant wrung her hands in despair. Clarissa Grant, the only missing bridesmaid, was throwing a spanner in the works.

Jane jerked her head around towards her mother, "It's no good, Clarissa has to get her leg set or something. She can't be walking in the wedding with a boot on..." Her eyes alighted on Katharine, and after a pause, "Katie, darling, you must be free next week and be one of my bridesmaids. Tatler is here to do a photoshoot. Come join us. We have a dress that will fit you."

By a Japanese garden set-up, a discreet distance from the photoshoot with people pretending to not eavesdrop, and Lady Hampton brightly buttonholing Marc, the two cousins were engaged in a somewhat heated discussion. Waving one hand and a wad of sodden tissues to her puffy eyes with the other, the Honorable Jane Smith-Brantley was winding herself up. "Oh, for heaven's sake, Katharine dear, do say you will step in for Clarissa. We are all set up with the photographer and her dress. The blonde wig and extensions won't take but a few minutes. And the wedding will be a pleasant break from that hospital."

Katharine's well-spoken voice answered the distraught fiancée, "What makes you think I want to do you any favors, Jane? After all, you were quite beastly in purchasing Smith Hall."

"In the end, Katharine, it worked out in your favor, don't you think I forgot that. But let's turn the page. About the wedding, there won't be all that vulgar attention, you know. This is not a statement wedding; it is traditional with friends and family."

"When I didn't get a wedding invitation, I was scheduled on shift this entire week. Your invitation must have been lost in the Royal Mail."

"Right, let's be truthful! No, Katie, you were not invited to the wedding because St Martin-in-the-Fields cannot hold more than 800 people. After all, you are family; we can see each other any time. But the others have to clear their calendars and fly in and it is only polite to put them at the top," Jane dismissed.

"The off-duty is already posted, Jane dear, so it is impossible for me with less than a week's notice for your hen-do and wedding rehearsal and the wedding. You will have to find someone else who can fit into Clarissa's bridesmaid dress. That is after all why you called me."

"You make it sound so easy, Katharine! No one else in my circle is outsize."

Katharine Smith-Brantley looked down upon herself. Even the printed pink full-skirted dress could conceal her womanly figure. Unlike the women on her late father's side of the family, who dieted fiercely, Katharine also had a bosom to be proud of. "Ah, now, *Janie,* because you are being candid, I will leave you and know that Aunt Beatrice will make it work out. I have to go back to my stroll now. Good luck to you and Prince Johnny."

"Wait, wait, Katharine, I give up. What do you want? I only have four days till the wedding rehearsal and I want this settled. You replacing Clarissa, what exactly do you want?"

Jane might be preoccupied with her royal wedding in London but her gardening and landscaping career taught her to see life as full of bargaining opportunities to get her way.

Marshalling her nerves, Katharine knew she had only a minute to propose outrageous terms. She was not bowled over by royalty, and was not eager to participate in this year's royal wedding. But Cousin Jane did not need to know that. "For starters, you cover all my expenses for the next week. Meals, taxis..."

"Easily done. All the bridesmaids are staying in town."

"Not just Clarissa's bridesmaid's dress, also rehearsal, reception and shoes and hotels..."

Vinegar-ly, Jane intoned, "But of course, I can't have you wear a couture bridesmaid dress on the Tube."

Bluntly, as if she were not interrupted, Katharine continued, "I do not want this nine-day favor to be taken out of my annual vacation."

"My, my, as if you need to pinch pennies with the cash you extorted for Smith Hall! Fine, I will have to enlist Papa to deal with that."

"Your Papa has always been willing to pick up the phone for you and your brothers." Katharine replied, drily. "No wig, this is my hair and I won't go for fake. And I want an invitation for Mama, your late uncle's wife."

"A simple oversight..."

"I never thought of you as simple-minded, Janie... And I insist that we shall both have seating and family photo positioning as befits your family and we attend all your receptions."

"What else?" Jane snapped.

"Hmmm, you can send some of the staff from Brantley House to the dower house to help Mama pack. You will be glad to pay for the shipping and rebook her in first class to Aunt Emma's."

"You know I am only doing this..."

"Because you had temporarily turned into Bridezilla and want to make amends." Katharine replied, generously, "You and Johnny have Smith Hall free and clear, Mum and I have paid our debts, thanks very much, and now we will present a civil united front to the world of Tatler!"

CHAPTER EIGHT

Dress to Impress...

The little twittering designer's assistant had been distraught,

"I am not a miracle worker."

"My cousin is a size 12, just like Clarissa," intoned Jane.

"There is size 12 and then there is size 12 couture for a unique woman. The top is satin, not much give, and the skirt... I can let out only so much..."

"Oh, put Katie in some Spanx or a girdle..."

Katharine sighed silently and swallowed her impatience. The other five bridesmaids were blonde, ethereal, and lissome. Even Clarissa normally fit like a glove into whatever her coterie from school wore but then she and her husband were expecting their first child. One had to make allowances for that.

The Principal Nursing Officer made arrangements for the leave, aware that the presence of St. Hedwig's at the royal wedding was a marketing and fundraising opportunity. Such short notice meant her staff nurse had to work until a couple nights before the wedding. Katharine had finished her last night shift, and then the day of appointments began. An immediate dash to a morning bridesmaid dress fitting, then to the flat, and off to the vet's for Coenraad's checkup. The vet bill will not matter, the most important thing was his kittenish eyesight!

Afterwards, outside on the pavement of the exclusive designer workroom, Jane withdrew her mobile phone from her understated and expensive beige leather handbag, "My driver will take you now to your flat to get your bags and cat. Do you really need to bring your cat?"

"For the next two weeks, I won't have my friends inconvenienced. Coenraad needs five more days of his medication."

Jane rolled her eyes, "You always were one for animals, cousin. If you would put the cat in a nice kennel..."

"Well, I won't," responded Katharine firmly as the family chauffeur pulled up beside the cousins.

"You will share a nice suite... see you at the rehearsal. You will be picked up at 4 PM," airkissed Jane as she stepped into her own Mini.

Katherine recognized Mr. Drake, her grandfather's, brother's, and now her uncle's driver. "There now, Miss Katharine, how nice to lay eyes on you again, and in your nurse uniform no less!" The grandfatherly man drove without a nerve through South Kensington out to the East End. "Master Edward's old flat, I'll be bound. Many a time I helped cover up for some hijinks at the UCL," he chuckled.

Katherine leant forward in the Rover, always happy to hear about her much-loved late brother.

In no time, with her bag in the boot and Coenraad's basket in the back seat, they sped off to Dr. Gibbs.

"Please enjoy a cup of coffee," the autocratic Dr. Gibbs directed Mr. Drake, "we won't be long." Then her softer side emerged as she examined the preening kitten.

Coenraad resigned himself for another round of 'ouchies' associated with his veterinarian, the microchipping, the rabies vaccine, the de-worming treatment, the eye pokes, and other indignities. Nevertheless, he was always ready to put on a good show. He hopped, mewed, opened his eyes, butted his head, and had on his best Sunday manners. The entire staff was proud of his progress, no one happier than his mama.

At the end of it all, Dr. Gibbs popped Coenraad into his basket and Katharine pocketed his documentation and his European Pet Passport. Her stomach growling, she was ready to go to the hotel and enjoy lunch and nap. Being the first to arrive, she was checked in by an obsequious concierge at the famed Carlos Place hotel and escorted upstairs by a retinue carrying her luggage. Inside the cat basket, Coenraad was making loud plaintive kitten noises. To the staff, these sounded like the discontented snarls of a lion-in-miniature.

It was a divine apartment with comfortable sitting room overlooking the city, doors connecting each bedroom room, ensuite baths, large enough to accommodate an entourage of bridesmaids or a family. The concierge staff helpfully directed her to one room with 2 double beds, for herself and her mother. Coenraad cautiously explored the room, finding it adequate. Katharine sniffed the fresh flowers in the enormous Louis XV vase, appreciating the scent of roses wafting through the room, and set about unpacking.

"I overheard Mama and Mrs. Drew talking that you entertained a nice young woman for breakfast..." the pretty Dutchwoman false-casually mentioned as they sat in the drawing room overlooking the Little Venice canal.

"I am just being kind to a staff nurse who found a kitten." He replied this statement by his sister, glowering into his Scotch whisky. He was not ready to reveal his hand but it seems word spreads fast from his household to his family.

Most people would have taken the hint and changed the topic of discussion. Many households were chattering about the upcoming royal wedding, to which Marc and Rienetta were guests of the groom's. Only his youngest sister, Rienetta, always loquacious and strong-willed Rienetta, the pet of the family, blithely ignored hints and warnings.

Indeed, she had been the only one of the family to boldly confront him on their collective unease about his impending marriage at that fateful Sint Nikolaus gathering over a decade ago... In a memorable scene, she took Marc to task for refusing to make a marriage settlement, calling him willfully blind and stupidly stubborn. She then persisted by airing her opinion about his religious intentions, "It will do you no good to change your religion for her. You were born a Calvinist and you will always be a Calvinist."

Chastened, he escorted Miriam in her white lace jumpsuit to the Amsterdam Gemeentehuis, as a proud member of the Reformed Church. They hosted a grand reception at the Hotel Amstel, with guests jetting in from all corners of the world. The couple then flew to St Bart's for a month-long honeymoon on private islands, yachts, and non-stop party invitations. Tall and tanned and young and wealthy, they returned to Europe ready to change the world.

Unfortunately, Miriam refused to learn Dutch, seeing it as a pointless use of her energies since Marc was spending a considerable amount of the time at St. Hedwig's. Truth be told, London was a bigger pond, across the pond, to make a splash on the international scene. It was littered with all manner of NGOs and charities du jour and the usual blonde-streaked and shrieked public school set.

On his scarce periods of free time, Marc realized to his dismay that he had been utterly infatuated with the idea of a unconventional choice of bride. Moreover, he had unrealistically expected her to fall in love with rural country life in Friesland. But she was always not available when Marc went to visit assorted family members in the northernmost province of his country.

They were at loggerheads on this issue whenever they argued, which was not often, as their paths seldom crossed. He was preoccupied attending to his patients at clinics, doing shifts at various hospitals, lecturing all over northern Europe.

She was in and out of Heathrow, as the title of 'baroness' coupled with her strikingly glamorous looks made good copy for the media. Championing paediatric issues that were her husband's specialization led Miriam to associated high-profile sport fundraisers for children and other attendant causes. Somehow, maybe deliberately, her schedule of goodwill ambassador work prevented her from joining in Thoe van der Veer family celebrations at Sint Nikolaus, Christmas, and New Year's Day...

Things came to a head over children just as Marc was heading to the ferry for a December crammed with work at medical schools and hospitals all over the Netherlands. Marc insisted on any future children being raised Dutch Calvinist, 'the Thoe van der Veers are Reformed Church, regardless of the faith of their mother' he bluntly stated. If that was good enough for Queen Máxima, it was good enough for Miriam.

It was not to her liking at all.

Marc came to his awakening, a guilty realization that this kind of marriage was not to his liking either. And Miriam could see how ill-suited they were too. In her travels, she could feel the pull of a wider horizon other than the wife to a homebody paediatrician. Shortly before Christmas, she already was filing the paperwork in London, the divorce capital of Europe, and had engaged a battery of QCs.

"What was the name of that Beatle singer who did not have a pre-nup?" asked Oom Walle, humorously, in a secret meeting of family elders the fortnight before Marc's wedding. The family had worked against the clock meticulously and ruthlessly to protect their property in a complicated series of trusts, in effect, cutting Marc loose. Family is family but fools have no claim on family assets. In the event of marital breakdown, Marc was to pay for any divorce settlement from his own personal capital, not his family's.

Before Marc's legal team could respond to the divorce petition, Miriam and other worthies of the global charity circuit jetted off to California. A reality show appearance on a flotilla of yachts off the Pacific coast was an exciting way to spend Christmas. A sudden storm came up, something went tragically wrong, and Marc was left a widower at the age of 27.

He flew out for the funeral and the burial at sea, saved from a costly divorce by the hand of Providence.

Although he was emotionally drained by his two year marriage, Marc did not swear off women. Once bitten, twice shy, Marc kept company with a succession of beauties of the SW1. He avoid remarriage, having adopted a rather glib motto, "If it ain't Dutch, it ain't much..."

His own family, however, continued to watch him like an egg on the verge of hatching something particularly nasty. His uncles and aunts, his older cousins, those who had witnessed his rebellious youth, were unable to forget their financial narrow escape. Those of his own generation had watched him indulge in 'poking them in the eye' and learnt from his mistake, his younger brother especially. For the subsequent generation, he was a living breathing object lesson of the penalty of youthful arrogance.

He marveled at Providence. For all these months, he had resisted the pull of Kathy, wary of making another match with a foreigner. In the end, he could not resist her kindness, his feelings, their compatibility, and was ready to take a chance again. And how he was rewarded, his dear Kathy is a half-Dutchwoman! Just who he needed in his lonely life.

He was enjoying his courtship. When the time was right, he would be presenting Kathy with the family engagement ring he had in the safe.

It was a sunny June day, perfect for a summer wedding and picture perfect for a royal wedding. From all corners of the city, media and monarchists and social media bloggers were emerging en masse from the buses and Tube stations for Trafalgar Square. Some had made a complete weekend out of it, attending the theatre the previous night, followed by Chinese food, and clubbing. Of all the places in the city, this central London square serves as a gathering spot on any day of the week, where church and art and people meet.

John Nash designed it as a tribute to Nelson's victory at Trafalgar, positively drenching the place with symbols to the Admiral with the famous lions, fountains, and the column in the centre. Surrounding these tributes to the national hero are the National Gallery, the National Portrait Gallery, and the gleaming white classical Greek temple structure of the Church of St. Martin-in-the-Fields. For today, it is not parishioners or tourists taking in the perfect acoustics, but the invited guests of Jane and Prince Johnny.

A little-known fact is this is a parish church for members of royal family – this meant that Prince Johnny and Jane could be wed there without going through the stringent requirements of other engaged couples. Straight from Buckingham Palace up the Mall, the royal carriages rode in military precision through the Admiralty Arch to a splendid halt in front of the church. Although the massive square was hosting a huge number of people celebrating the wedding, the cheers hardly disturbed with the calm demeanor of the young prince as he alighted and saluted the crowd stretching all the way to Canada House.

By now standing next to the Archbishop, Prince Johnny barely heard the occasional quip from his chief supporter, The Honorable Francis Everley. "You doing very well, waiting for your bride is just like us staking out those hobbys."

The Prince grimaced at his friend, "I would like to be there when you to tell Jane to her face that you compare her to bird-watching in the Romney Marsh."

"Erm, 'we' compare her, not just I!"

"Well, 'Frankie Farmer', why don't you just...?"

The Archbishop cleared this throat, "Gentlemen..." to be muffled by the organ thundering the hymn, "Be Thou My Vision".

And she was a vision as a bride, thought Lady Hampton, as she turned to see Jane, on the arm of her father, Lord Hampton, walking down the nave in her two-inch embellished lace and satin pumps. Jane's A-line chiffon wedding gown with a bodice of finely beaded tulle, dropped waistline, gently gathered chiffon skirt, cap sleeves with a short chapel train and the mid-length veil from her mother, would have looked just as appropriate had the wedding ceremony been conducted by the vicar at the village church close to Brantley House.

Seated in her embroidered pastel aubergine coat dress and mother-of-the-bride hat, Aunt Beatrice breathed in a satisfied sigh. The music was splendid as befitting St Martin-in-the-Fields.

Katharine feeling encased in the vice of a dress slowly followed the line of young women serving as bridesmaids, she was the last in line and suppressed the urge to smile at her mother as she passed that lady, who was in an understated summery green past-the-knee length dress with a modest scoop neckline and wide, flowingly 3/4 sleeves. The ruffle fabric at the hem gave Mrs. Smith-Brantley a small European flair. The photographers and camera people desultorily tracked the shot of the bridesmaids ahead of her, looking like the corps de ballet from La Bayadere, all the same creamy complexions, their blonde hair in low buns, not a strand out of place, with their rose-blush gowns.

Gasps dropped from the television and internet streaming viewers of the wedding in the church of St Martin-in-the-Fields as the camera panned from the porch to the nave. Katharine Smith-Brantley's shapely self was silhouetted cleanly by the sunlight. It was modest and modern, with three-quarter sleeves. The rose blush couture dress was full length, a lace front with no stretch, which made Katharine's bosom take on a massive appearance. The slight mermaid skirt tailoring was about half size too small.

"Blimey, that is bootilicious!" the Daily Mail announcer burped out, "Get me the name of that bridesmaid!"

Leafing through the official Palace announcement, the intern read aloud, "It says here 'Miss Katharine Smith-Brantley', right, the cousin, and sister of the late Lord Hampton, she replaced Clarissa Grant."

"Well, grant me some wishes. This Brantley is beyond Rear of the Year, there's so much on display that we have the Brantley B&B: Booty and Boobs!" tittered the presenter, awed at his attempt at bawdy humor.

During the wedding ceremony and the afternoon reception, the well-behaved guests respected the rule against social media. At the Palace, everyone engaged in lighthearted conversation while the royal family gathered in the garden for the last of the official photos. Marc steered his sister over to Katharine and her mother, making introductions, "Mrs. Smith-Brantley and her daughter, Katharine, fresh from bridesmaid duties."

"You looked so cool and collected, even with the television cameras and an audience in the millions!" smiled Rienetta.

"Just well-trained, we have to pretend to be unflappable in the A&E, although inside we are quaking with fright," laughed Katharine.

"Oh, are you the staff nurse with the kitten?" Rienetta avoided Marc's side-eye, "I hear from Mrs. Drew that the kitten is just the thing!"

"He certainly takes all our free time. A little changeling, he no longer wants just milk. It is tuna he craves. And so much energy, our little man makes things sparkle by running into the vases. Kevin is such a dear to keep cleaning up after Coenraad."

"So convenient when your housemate is also a handyman," nodded Mrs. Smith-Brantley, handing around champagne from a passing waiter.

Heavy security kept the tabloids away from the delectables as the guest sat down for lunch. The menu for the reception highlighted the finest of the British Isles- Scottish salmon, English beef, Welsh salt marsh lamb, and organic vegetables and fruit from the groom's kitchen garden. All these were washed down by wines from Australia, Canada, and the Everley chateaux.

"We can give you a lift back to your hotel," chatted Rienetta to Katharine, "I am flying home tomorrow, and Drew can drive your mother and me to the airport. She's in First Class? The airline won't mind changing so we can share the same flight."

In a manner like her brother's, of knowing what can be done shall be done, Rienetta looked satisfied, "Now isn't this nice, Marc?"

With a slow day on the news-front, the hashtag #BrantleyB&B was already trending on social media. The UK tabloids analyzed close-ups of Katharine's backside and magnificent bosom. Their American counterparts and TV reality show doctors debated 'has she or hasn't she' butt enhancement surgery and implants. By 3 PM, the time Prince Johnny and 'Our Princess Jane' drove off for their honeymoon as the realm's newest duke and duchess, #BrantleyB&B was going viral.

CHAPTER NINE

Mail at Work

THE A&E DEPARTMENT WAS THE FIRST AT ST. HEDWIG'S to examine a fake patient. "The British public wants the inside scoop of being nursed by Brantley B&B..." whined the first reporter thrown off the premises by two burly orderlies. The tabloid press had been off-track for about 24 hours, looking for a Nurse Smith-Brantley. Until this enterprising bloodhound tried 'Staff Nurse Smith', and hit the jackpot.

Katharine was never so relieved to take a night shift, leaving St. Hedwig's under the protection of the shadowy dawn skies. She hastened to the basement flat and thankfully shut the door behind her, leaning in gratitude for an ordinary busy evening.

Coenraad, the rambunctious, came up to her intent on showering her with some early morning feline affection. She picked him up, let him drape over her shoulder, and softly patted his furry little body. Yawning, she crept into her bedroom and fell asleep instantly, with the kitten curled up beside her.

After her sleep, Katharine proceeded to wash her hair and mull over other tasks before her next shift. With her hair in towel turban, she did her nails and made a list of items to stock up the larder. On the way back from the local green grocers, she took a call on her mobile phone from Marc. "A day out in the country, to check on the dower house on my next day off...?" She looked around the shabby East End neighbourhood, "Yes, please!"

In a dreamworld, Katharine barely noticed how she carried home and unpacked the Vim, the Persil, baked beans, the eggs, and the cans of tomatoes

When she later showed up for her shift, her team reported promptly to the nurse -in-charge at A&E. Leslie beckoned to her, "I have seen the front page of The Daily Mail," holding up the front page with a blurry photo of her in the A&E from the previous night.

The heading blared: 'Brantley B&B: The full-figured woman who smiles with good teeth, someone you can take home to your Nan and not have to explain things like a pink hair, black nail varnish, and tattoos on her ass.'

She groaned, this was not a good sign. She knew it would be a 5-day wonder and then everyone will go back to talking about Manchester United or the Six Nations Rugby or some other Hollywood star. With Cousin Jane and Prince Johnny on honeymoon, they were out of it.

By the middle of her shift, she was not sure how celebrities dealt with the limelight. St. Hedwig's was besieged by all manner of aggressive reporters intercepting departing patients and visitors, calling on registrars, house doctors, consultants, and even masquerading as nurses!

The board of governors convened an emergency meeting off-site, calling in additional security to manage the bedlam with their staff already stretched to the breaking point with their regular duties.

The porter, Mr. Reynolds, greeted Katharine from her break with a message. "The Principal Nursing Officer asks to see you."

"Wonder what that is about," she mused, heading to that august lady's office.

Looking like a briefcase-carrying executive who had never seen a sluice room in her life, the middle-aged Principal Nursing Officer, Lygia Wilson, invited Katharine to sit down, "Staff Nurse Smith, your participation in the royal wedding has brought a degree of attention to this hospital. Although we are thankful for the publicity to our work, the media are becoming a nuisance in the A&E."

She pursed her lips in contempt, "They are compromising our patient care and interfering with the smooth running of St. Hedwig's. The board of governors had an emergency meeting on it. We have enough on our plates without all number of faux admissions to A&E just since breakfast."

"What I am proposing is that you go on paid leave till this entire thing blows over." She looked at her watch, "If you hand over an hour before your shift ends, you can get a headstart on leaving the premises..."

Her eyes round with astonishment, Katharine knew there was no time to lose. She texted her flatmates to expect her in two hours as she rushed back to the A&E.

The Professor was pushing the Rolls Royce to its limits. At the teleconference of the Board of Governors, they all agreed to put Staff Nurse Smith-Brantley on leave with immediate effect. That was the extent of their concern for her for they quickly turned their attention back to their hospital responsibilities. But Marc did not like to leave Kathy at the mercy of the tabloid hyenas.

On his car phone, he called Daniels & Gilbank, "Miss Gilbank, you have seen the tabloids, Miss Smith-

Brantley cannot stay in London... Can you arrange for Mrs. Dean at the dower house...?"

As luck would have it, a multiple vehicle crash filled up A&E, pressing as many staff as possible to triage and treat the victims. The Professor, appearing out of nowhere, lent his expertise to a grateful overworked crew. Katharine went about A&E as efficiently as possible, directing junior nurses, raiding the cupboards for bandages. Then she looked at the clock and began easing herself out. Beyond tired, she caught Marc's glance and the unmistakable motion of his head, towards the staff exit. Almost at the screaming point herself, she grabbed her satchel and headed in that direction.

Marc met up with her, and took her elbow, "I know all about it, we had the board meeting..."

"Oh, yes, I forgot you are on the board..."

He ushered her into the car without hesitation, "We have to stay ahead of those tabloid jackals. Can we go to your flat and pack a few items and then get you to the dower house? Now that it is yours, and behind royal security gates, you should be safe there."

Kevin Dickenson was up when Marc and Katharine arrived, "I just chased off that Daily Mail bloke too. He almost charged the door but Coenraady here scratched him ruddy screaming." He looked out onto the street, "They seemed to be gone... for now."

As Katharine scooped up the purring kitten, looking like butter wouldn't melt in his tiny mouth.

Paul was fit to be tied, "Those nasty tabloid reporters, the Sun online today, have this here article."

What Kevin pulled up on his tablet was the headline 'Brantley B&B is where she pulls! A Basement & Brothel --where men are in and out, all hours of the day and night.

"It quotes those teenage NEETs down the street. Bloody liars...!" Kevin fumed.

The Daily Mail led off with 'With an attack cat, BrantleyB&B is a wild and rollicking place.'

"I shall pursue legal action," fumed Katharine, "I am going to pack right now, Marc, I have very little, please give me ten minutes."

The three men shook hands, "I shall be on my guard with Staff Nurse, never fear," intoned Marc. The other two agreed this was the best action to take, the Rolls Royce was a good vehicle to spirit Katharine out of the capitol.

Once in the car, with her modest bags and the cat basket, Marc steered through the quiet streets heading towards Warminster while Katharine kept up with the tabloids on her mobile phone. "Talk about trash! Oh, they are making insinuations all over the place...!

"And look, they have also interviewed Kevin's wife!"

Apparently, Kevin's wife had called up the Daily Mail and screamed about the Sun reporting staff for insinuating a love nest. "My husband is a decent man trying to support his family. This London is too *feckin'* expensive for us to live in. He comes home all worn out. Not enough nurses on staff. Who can train to be nurse when the bloody fools at Westminster charge 9,500 pounds annual tuition?"

Marc's face was inscrutable, trying not to grin, "Well, at least you have character witnesses."

Katharine laughed, "I should be in tears." Then she scrolled some more, "Good heavens, they even have a live feed from the gates of Smith Hall."

At once, they knew the press would be an obstacle to the dower house.

Marc turned to Katharine, "You do know what Plan B is?"

"What do you have in mind?"

"I have more than enough petrol for the morning ferry from Harwich..."

Katharine squeaked, "To Hoek van Holland?"

He looked closely at her, "Just so."

CHAPTER TEN

Huis Rules

THE FIRST free breath Katharine took in 24 hours was while watching the coast of England get brighter and brighter and further and further away as the morning car ferry steamed ahead to Europe. She and the Professor made their way from London with him steering past the morning commuters like an experienced coach driver. Indeed, he had become very familiar with the route over the years. Katharine, as a hands-free passenger, did her part, reserving their tickets online on her mobile phone. Flush with cash from the sale of Smith Hall, she felt carefree at the cost of last-minute reservations. Marc was not pleased at the refusal of his credit card for payment but there was not much he could do as his attention was fully occupied with the road.

They arrived at Harwich in plenty of time, almost an hour before the ferry was open for motor vehicles and foot passengers to board. Prudently taking the little

kitten out for his breakfast and then for a trot, Katharine administered his eye drops, and popped him back into the basket. "You have plenty of water and air, Coenraad, in this airy car," she coaxed the kitten to sleep. "Next time, we get you a kennel." Marc took great satisfaction at that remark as he started the car.

They drove onto the superferry once the crew permitted boarding and took care of the formalities regarding Coenraad's first visit to the European mainland. Then Katharine and Marc headed to the cabin deck. Giddy with anticipation, Katharine was looking forward to sleeping soundly. In previous ferry rides with her family, they had always travelled at night and stayed in inside berths which were comfortable enough. But a real bed with outside window views during the day was an extravagance. Although Katharine was sure she would fall asleep the minute her head hit the pillow and miss the view of the sea...

She placed her handbag on the stateroom table and turned to Marc, "Thank you so much for getting us out. It should blow over in a few days, and I can get back to work."

He kissed her cheek, "You have been a tower of strength for your mother. And very gracious to your cousin. I know you are dead on your feet, so first some breakfast before the ship sets sail or your growling stomach will waken you in a couple hours…" Marc yawned too, a gleam in his tired eyes, "We can catch up on our rest soon."

While waiting for their sausages and eggs breakfast and hot fresh rolls to be served by the friendly waitress, Katharine updated her mother through text message, ending with "What an adventure so far."

Marc poured her a glass of fresh orange juice, "It will be late when we dock at the Hook. I suggest we head straight to my sister Rienetta's near Bolsward. Tomorrow morning, we can drive you to your aunt's."

Nicely full with food, and overwhelmed by fatigue, Katharine brushed her teeth and slipped into her nightie. Looking like a little girl, Katharine's happy countenance drew Marc almost beyond the boundaries of propriety. He bestowed a kiss which she found very appealing indeed. After she leisurely returned his affections, he closed the curtains on the seaview, turned off the light, and went to his own cabin. As she slipped away into a deep slumber, Katharine mused, "I shall awaken speaking Dutch."

By mutual agreement, they changed languages upon disembarking, her Dutch a bit rusty, his Frisian a bit wild. Their merriment made the 2 hour drive a bit of a relief from the heavy traffic on the A4, then skirting Schipol, and threading their way up the A9. Being almost summer, the sun was glowing, casting light on the densely populated southern provinces as they raced from the Hook to the north. In the boot were their overnight bags and her uniform, not to see the light of day on this escapade. In the backseat mewed an anxious Coenraad, uneasy to be so long confined inside his basket.

Twenty minutes across the Afsluitdijk, they emerged in Friesland, the wide horizon hardly touched by puffy clouds. The rural north of the country sped by in a blur as Marc drove through the few towns and farms in the province the intensely patriotic Frisians call Fryslân.

Passing Bolsward, the Rolls Royce turned onto a smaller road for a few kilometers of farmland. These gave way to a few houses and shops gathered around a large austere church. A quick turn and the car cruised on a rural lane with a high wall, then turned into open gates. Straight as a yardstick, the drive ended at the solid wooden doors to a stately gentleman's residence. Three stories high, it looked 16th century, solid and self-assured. Katharine could glimpse a garden and barns in the back of the gabled house.

Her hostess wrenched open the door not one second after Marc pulled under the huge portico. "I have been looking out the drawing room window for ages," raced Rienetta down the steps. As Katharine climbed out the car, Marc holding open the door, Rienetta gave them both a welcoming hug.

Ever eager to please, two dogs followed her, Charlie, the well-mannered golden retriever and Max, a little dog with long ears and a foxy tail, insinuated his tiny body into the car and barked his head off in welcome at Coenraad.

Rienetta prudently reached in for Coenraad's basket and led the way inside. "I have a wonderful surprise for you, Katharine," she smiled with innocently-wide eyes at her brother. "I drove your mother and Aunt Emma to stay overnight too!

"They are napping in their rooms and Father and Mother are dressing. We have an hour before supper."

Marc was suddenly aware of being royally stitched up something serious. He sighed to his sister, "What are you up to?"

She demurred, "Whatever do you mean? Good old-fashioned Dutch hospitality..."

Just inside the main doorway, a dapperly dressed middle-aged man in staff uniform made his unhurried way across the massive hallway with its black and white tiles. "Kathy, let me introduce you to Jan, our good friend, and his wife, Touke," Marc clapped the family's mainstay, "Juffrouw Smith-Brantley speaks Frisian." The majordomo face was immediately wreathed in smiles as the local language was employed by all.

Rienetta linked arms with Katharine as Marc carried the cat basket, "Come with me to the kitchen, Coenraad, and Katharine, I shall show you to your room after we get him settled."

The Professor gave Jan the keys to the boot of the car, "Yes, yes, by all means, Coenraad must meet our resident cat. Queenie will make much of him."

Queenie, as it turned out, was not inclined to make anything at all of the kitten who leaped impetuously out of his basket. She looked regally down at the interloper, her stately black-and-white tail swinging in distain. Which only encouraged Coenraad to pull out all the stops to ingratiate himself. To no avail.

Coenraad's discouraged head tucked into her bosom, Katharine stroked his dear ears, "Well, we are only visiting," said Katharine comfortingly.

"We'll see..." said the Professor under his breath, then he coughed to cover his words.

Touke obligingly brought the visiting feline a saucer of milk and tuna. They left the kitchen as the black kitten forgot his disappointment, quickly burying his head into a bowl of food.

Rienetta danced in excitement, "We held back dinner, you need a glass of something after the long drive," as she led Katharine up the imposing stairs that led to a gallery three sides. Dramatically she threw open a door halfway down a corridor leading from the gallery. "This is your room with its own ensuite bathroom. Your mother and aunt are next door. Take your time, I am going to dress. See you in the drawing room in 60 minutes."

It was a very pretty room with a balcony overlooking the gardens in the back of the house. Thick Turkish rugs of some antiquity were laid strategically throughout the room, matched by thick curtains tied back from the tall windows. Two comfortable armchairs grouped around a table, with a portrait of some 18th century ancestress of Rienetta overlooking a dressing table with a triple mirror and a four-poster bed somehow filled with room without looking like an antique store.

The sound of a gentle knock and the creak of the door brought two middle-aged women into the room. "Tante Emma, Mama...!" cried Katharine as the three ladies reunited as if they had not seen each other in a decade.

Mrs. Smith-Brantley perched herself on the bed, agog for all the details of eluding the paparazzi. "Rienetta called to invite us over and even drove over herself to pick us up."

"I have your old room all ready for you, so quiet," Aunt Emma, in a brown midi-length dress trimmed with burgundy and sturdy two-inch heels to give her diminutive self some height, hugged her, "You will not want to leave Fryslân."

Katharine giggled, "Please don't tempt me. I have to go back to St. Hedwig's."

Aunt Emma looked at her sister, "I thought with the sale of Smith Hall, Katharine, that you are now a woman of means and also a woman of property..."

Looking at Katharine, her mother replied, "That is true, Emma," she gazed pensively, "My daughter does not need to return to London, though I think my daughter prefers to return to St. Hedwig's."

Jan the butler opened the double doors leading to the drawing room. Just putting down her knitting was a kindly homely middle aged woman with Rienetta's smile. A much older man rose from his large armchair near the fireplace. It was evidently Marc's father, this would be Marc in forty years. "Welcome to Huis Thoe."

"Thank you for putting back dinner for us. It was the first time for me to use the Euro pet passport for Coenraad…"

The Baroness looked inquisitive, "We are most pleased. But who is this Coenraad?"

"It is the name that Marc chose for my new kitten." answered Katharine, as she then turned to Marc to ask, "How did you know Coenraad would respond to the name 'Coenraad'?"

Their son explained, "It is a custom in my family that the first-born take on one of the names of his Thoe van der Veer grandfather. I have always been partial to your name, Vader, 'Coenraad', it was a whim on my part."

The Baron Coenraad Thoe van der Veer threw back his elderly head and roared with laughter.

Over a dinner with damask table linens, high-backed chairs around a table that could seat a dozen, Katharine made mannerly conversation with her hosts and Rientta's fiancé, Sarre. Not unlike Brantley House, portraits of long-deceased Thoe van der Veers presided over the smoked salmon, beef au jus, salad, and poached pear. The Baron and the Baroness may live in a home without Wi-Fi; however they kept up with the times.

The conversation continued in the drawing room about the splendid music at Jane's wedding, some of the more outlandish hats, and laughed off the tabloid articles. For Katharine and her mother, this was the first time in years that they felt totally relaxed.

"Before breakfast, Kathy," murmured Marc, "I usually ride, would you like to join me? We have a mare that Rienetta usually rides... you will find her as ladylike as you."

Rienetta, sitting beside Sarre, objected, "Now Marc, I have..." Then she thought better, and turned on a sweet smile, "I have, um, thought that we all could ride at Sarre's family home." She beamed at how she improvised.

The mid-thirties chestnut-haired fiancé indulged Rienetta's swift change of topic, and gamely played along with it. Like his own father, an orthopedic surgeon, Sarre was a country man at heart. The elder Professor and his English wife had spent most of their married life in their country house outside of Groningen raising their children and still make it their home. "We three grew up there, nothing makes Mama more at home than the garden and the stables. Although we like our house in England very much too, it was our great-grandmother's.

"We only started using the house in Groningen when we started medical school, Thomas and I. Our older half-brother and half-sister had already moved out to a flat in Rotterdam and so we had free rein. While you are here, my family will want to meet you, Katharine."

He was a splendid foil for Rienetta's tall blonde looks, thought Katharine, and just as good natured. Rienetta went on, "In one week, we can put a dent into Groningen! I can take you anywhere you want."

"Dutch pastry shops, most of all! I have almost forgotten how to enjoy food beyond the grounds of St. Hedwig's."

Aunt Emma looked fondly at her niece, "We will hardly see you, my dear, you know all the best cake shops and tea rooms on this side of the Afsluitdijk." To the assembled people, she elaborated about the red-faced Katharine, "Katharine stayed with me during her Erasmus year and the course afterwards. The bicycle came in handy for both exercise and transportation!"

After the kind laughter died down, Katharine decided herself ready to retire for the night.

The next morning, as Marc promised, the mare Daisy was to her liking. As they ambled through the fields beyond the Huis Thoe parkland, he probed her off-days, "I have tickets for that new exhibition at the National Gallery you wanted to see. It opens in three weeks."

"How lovely of you, Marc. I think some football WAG will put on an outrageous hat at Ascot and the tabloids will be done with Brantley B&B. Two weeks tops and I am back at St. Hedwig's."

"About the rest of the English summer season... Wimbledon interest you? Perhaps Henley?"

Katharine wriggled her nose, "I would rather play tennis or plant things than watch some people I don't even know. How about a picnic at the dower house? I can bake some scones with homemade jam and little sausages and cut some sandwiches."

"I find myself thinking this could be a most marvelous summer, Kathy. At the end of it all, when you have gotten to know me better, and like the idea of a future together, I shall ask you when I can post the banns and you can give me an answer." He glanced at her searchingly. Katharine gave him a smile from the heart and nodded.

Watching the couple from the conservatory, the Baroness and Mrs. Smith-Brantley nodded in satisfaction.

Katharine woke up in her bed, stretching in its vastness. The brocade velvet curtains were drawn back, mild sunlight shimmering through the open window. Still half asleep, she was lying there breathing the air lightly scented by the blooms in Tante Emma's garden.

A whole week so far, she had eased into country living, gardening, arranging church flowers, sailing in Sneek with Marc, a last-minute fill-in at the local elder home...

One more week, and she was to return to St. Hedwig's. A frown and a deep sigh... for days she had been willing herself to come up with some degree of enthusiasm for city life and hospital work.

A cup of tea placed on the bedside table, even with her eyes closed, she could tell by her mother's quiet slippers.

A little plop by her side, it was kitten Coenraad, purring in her ears. She opened her eyes lazily. Unblinking, Coenraad looked at her through clear eyes. "Oh, you clever thing..."

He jumped off the bed and scampered after her mother through the door which was just opening...

To the St. Hedwig's A&E.

Katharine sobbed, "No, no, no... I can't."

"Wake up, Katharine, you are having a bad dream...!" She opened her eyes to her anxious mother holding in her arms a mewing Coenraad. And Marc bending over the hammock where Kathy had been napping that afternoon.

Katharine sat up, dry heaving, "I can't... " Marc took her into his arms and she rested her head on his shoulder, forgetting Mrs. Smith-Brantley. She sighed, "Marc, we have to talk..."

Her mother prudently left them, on the pretext of giving the suppertime potatoes a prod. Katharine leaned back on the cushion of a rattan settee, "I am not sure I am ready to return to London. I am not sure if I will ever want to return to St. Hedwig's." She looked intently at him, "But I would go back because you are there." She looked away, a bit embarrassed at being so frank.

Marc held her hand, "You do not need to nurse any more..."

"Because of the money? That is true but I trained to nurse and I will continue to nurse. Just not A&E any more, not mandatory shiftwork any more. I would be happy to nurse part time. That would be the minimum to keep up my state registration. I have seen nurses give it up and then have difficulty getting back in. That won't happen to me."

"I see... If you cannot stand the thought of returning to St. Hedwig's, dear, stay here. You won't be idle as a nurse."

"Marc, you do have a foot in two worlds as it were. The UK and the Netherlands..."

"My work is based in St. Hedwig's and lecturing. My only home is in Little Venice. An inheritance from an aunt as is the car. Here in the Netherlands, I stay with whichever family member feels generous," he looked thoughtfully at Katharine, "My salary is generous but you are the one with the means to pick and choose."

"Could you get work here in the Netherlands, Marc?"

"Most assuredly I could. But it would not be easy for you to get employment, it is quite a process. All employers in the Netherlands require healthcare professionals to be on the BIG registration, the Individual Healthcare Act (*Wet op de Beroepen in de Individuele Gezondheidszorg, BIG*)"

Katharine looked at him, "Oh, that. When I came over for the Erasmus exchange, I stayed on to qualify over here as well." She looked a bit smug, "Not many British nurses can demonstrate fluency in Dutch and Frisian. So yes, I am already on the BIG."

Marc gathered his Kathy closer, "Then what am I waiting for? You are going to be a most clever wife. How lucky I am.

"I have been carrying this around with me for a few days," He opened a little ring box, "Kathy, would you wear this ring? And make me the happiest man in the world."

He did not wait for an answer. Marc fitted the antique family engagement ring, two diamonds surrounding a central sapphire on a rose-gold band, onto her finger, and saluted each finger with a kiss.

She gave him the most radiant smile and raised her lips for his kiss, "Dearest Marc, you already make me happy so I should absolutely do the same for you."

Sitting in the garden with two weeks to go before her wedding, Katharine reflected on the past fortnight. It had not taken her long to find her ideal part time nursing job, one shift a week, enough to accumulate the number of hours every five years to remain on the BIG registry. Her fluency in English, Dutch, and Frisian stood her in good stead.

Which was good as she was soon caught up in organizing a wedding in just four short weeks. Everyone in the Thoe van der Veer family agreed on Marc's fine choice of bride. Help on arranging the civil ceremony, the church wedding, and reception, and clothes and guest lists came from all sides of the family.

Katharine also spent much time online and ambling along country roads looking for a house with garden, preferably not in town, for their family home. With the anticipated rents from letting out her dower house and his Little Venice home, Katharine calculated she and Marc could live quite comfortably and provide their future children with a good education.

Marc was still somewhat resistant to her purchasing a house, which she attributed to stubborn male pride. "What does it matter if I buy it and keep it in my name? There is no point in renting a flat when I have the means to buy a suitable home now. Roomy with a garden and a paddock for a couple ponies and a donkey too." She could be stubborn too.

Mrs. Smith-Brantley called from the sitting room, "Marc is phoning you, dear, on the landline."

He was calling from London, "Dearest, I contacted someone about paediatric work in Leeuwarden... and Groningen University also would like me to lecture..."

Dancing around the room, with her mother and clear-eyed Coenraad joining in on the celebration, Katharine was so proud of Marc. He was such a clever man, with many years of experience at St. Hedwig's. He could even set up a private practice, if he wanted. It was a dream come true that he has found well-paying and meaningful work in Friesland and can continue to lecture at various places needing his expertise.

Father and son were in the dark-panelled billiards room, desultorily circling each other, cues in hand and lobster thermidor inside their stomachs. Despite his great age, the head of the family held his own against his son, lining up his shots, grunting when the balls went where they were supposed to go, harrumphing when they had minds of their own.

"Your mother is very much looking forward to Sneek next week after your wedding, even though she does not have gardens such as this there."

Taking his lead from his father, Marc responded in good-humor, "Not a long drive at all for Mama." Marc had arrived from three weeks' wrapping up work in London in time for the wedding. He looked out the long windows overlooking the Dutch garden where the Baroness was strolling with her daughter and Kathy, "She can pick to her heart's content."

After a few minutes of strategic attention to the billiards table, their dinner jackets off, the Baron took his attention off his game, "With Rienetta getting married, this family home will be quieter. Much quieter..."

"A relief for you, no doubt," Marc chuckled.

The Baron took a long sip of his iced water, "It will be quieter when we move to Sneek..."

Marc almost missed his shot, "To the house in Sneek? Vader, you and Mama and the staff...?"

"Oh, we will take one or two of the staff with us," the Baron bent over, intent on a tricky shot to send two balls into the respective corners, "The rest could stay here, for the sake of the horses and the garden. The horses would not adapt well to the water." He chuckled at his attempt at humor. "Easy reach of Leeuwarden hospital and clinics. Perhaps you would like to move in...?"

Looking closely at his father, Marc sighed in resignation, "I do love and cherish the estate, but I do not have the income to maintain it..."

"No one does," interrupted the Baron.

At Marc's look asking for more information, the elderly man explained, "The family trust takes care of all our property holdings. Taxes, repairs, maintenance, staffing expenses, the roof..."

"And asset protection," added Marc, stiffly.

The Baron looked benevolently at his eldest son. "Exactly. And hasn't it turned out to everyone's benefit. I think Katharine would like this wedding present."

For Marc and his father, it was more than that. It was rapprochement.

CHAPTER ELEVEN

Not in the bedroom...

THE MASTER BEDROOM OF THE BARONS THOE van der Veer was quite comfortable, thought Katharine, as she settled herself amongst the pillows. Freshly bathed; her hair a cloud on her shoulders and an array of colourful pamphlets on her lap. Ports of call on their honeymoon.

They needed to rest up before departing tomorrow after breakfast for the cruise ship. "Unpack once, shore excursions, and waltzing under the stars," murmured Marc. The guests at the reception looked on approvingly, Aunt Emma telling his Oom Walle about the library at ancient Ephesus.

Katharine had begun that day much too early that morning. Too excited to lie about, she crept through the silent house to the back, picking fresh flowers from Aunt Emma's garden. This was her wedding day! When her mother and aunt finally tracked her down with her breakfast tray, the eggs were cool, the fruit plate was warm, and Coenraad had knocked over the bud vase in kittenish playfulness. Looking at the clock, it was a miracle that all would be put to rights before Marc came to meet her for the civil ceremony.

In his custom-made suit and shoes gleaming, Marc emerged from the Rolls looking handsome and distinguished. She had sighed as her heart turned over. He smiled at Katharine, extending his hand to her and kissing her cheek, "You look so beautiful."

Later after the short ceremony in the wedding chamber in the raadhuis, everyone proceeded in a leisurely merry fashion to the old church, to generations of the Thoe van der Veer. Accompanied by Mrs. Smith-Brantley, Aunt Emma, Jane, and Rienetta to a private room just off the main chapel, Katharine swiftly changed from the rather business-like deep pink dress with modest square neck long-sleeved and midi-length A-line skirt and hat of the civil ceremony into her bridal gown and the Brantley tiara for the religious wedding.

It was on loan from Uncle Michael, being taken out for air, so to speak, now twice in the space of two months. This act of family rapprochement hoovered up the misery of transporting the heirloom diamond-and-amethyst tiara across to the Netherlands. All the guests could see was how stunning it looked while perched above the bride's veil. The historic veil that had previously graced Jane's high bun was blonde lace with delicate embroidered roses with a distinct gold trim. Katharine's mousy curls, for once, were somewhat tamed into a semi low-bun framed her radiant face.

The Thoe van der Veer diamond-and-ruby drop earrings caught fire against the background of the gown's deceptive simplicity, an A-line gown of silk organza capped by a lace motif bodice, a wide embroidered waist band, and a modest v-neck neckline, and petal cap sleeve.

So intent were Katharine and Marc to make their way to the altar and the dominee that the couple was oblivious to the guests looking discreetly over their shoulders.

At the wedding luncheon, the eclectic menu was a nod to their guests from all over Europe - Norwegian smoked salmon, muskovy duck, osso bucco, paella valenciana, fruit freshly picked from the glasshouses on the estate. With each dish was a splendid selection of wines from the cellar.

Katharine's former flat-mates still lived in the basement flat and miraculously all had time off to attend the wedding. They were quite thrilled at being flown over on the chartered plane with Jane and Johnny and assorted other guests, celebrating their friend's change of circumstances. The Prince Edward County wine they brought over was also being offered. The best man's older half-brother, Sarel, who wandered from table to table taking photographs, in his prime had travelled the world for Vogue, camera in hand. Throughout the entire meal, champagne was drunk for the bridal couple's happiness, speeches were made, and the more exuberant guests made merry as they clinked their glasses.

A tinkling noise from the other side of the four-poster canopied bed brought Katharine out of her reverie. A glass carafe, two glasses, and one heirloom Ming dynasty vase being jostled was the source of the ominous noise.

"Coenraad..." she reprimanded the black fluff reaching for the tulip arrangement.

Obedient to his mistress's glance, the sleek black cat dexterously leapt from the bedside table onto her lap. He bounced three times and whirled cheerfully around in three circles. Regaining his balance, he snuggled up to the new baroness, butting his head against her creamy white laced nightie. She stroked his dear little head in forgiveness as he snuggled close. Coenraad preferred to play up being a kitten although he was starting to outgrow that phase of his life.

Not one minute later, the door to one of the bathrooms opened. Wearing a dressing gown of some magnificence, the professor paused, taking in the scene before him. Katharine smiled shyly at her husband. Alert in an instant, the cat sat up, looking at Marc unblinkingly. Territorial, his feline glare locks onto the groom's eyes.

Without a word, Marc scooped up the cat, affronted at this highhanded action. As Katharine laughed, her new husband opened the door to the sitting room of the bedroom suite, strolled through to the double doors to the hallway, and deposited the kitten neatly outside. The Baron closed the door firmly shut and turned around to rejoin his bride.

The young cat sat for a moment, taken aback by his inglorious ejection from the bridal suite. Coenraad pondered the situation, shook himself in a feline manner, then got onto his four paws, and with his tail in the air, went in search of Queenie.

CHAPTER TWELVE: EPILOGUE

The following August...

From the DailyMail.com website

THE FIRST CHILD BORN TO 'OUR PRINCESS JANE' and Prince Johnny of Wales, the Duke and Duchess of Glamis, was christened Phillip Albert James at the Music Room in Buckingham Palace on an unseasonably warm summer's day.

Despite Brexit, no fewer than three of the new royal's six godparents are from across the Channel. The Duc d'Anjou arrived for the ceremony, conducted by the Archbishop of Canterbury, shortly after stepping from the Eurostar. The Duke's fourth cousin, Herzogin Maria, flew in from Austria.

Bringing up the rear – 'Who can forget the spectacular BrantleyB&B at last year's wedding, lads? Not I!' – driving over from the estate in the Netherlands, the Duchess's first cousin, Baroness Thoe van der Veer, and her husband, the renown paediatric consultant, Professor Baron Marc Thoe van der Veer. The still-bootylicious former Katharine Smith-Brantley herself is a new mother of twins.

###

FEEDBACK

Mimi Laurence

Did you feel that the characters connected in this story?
Would you like a sequel?

Let me know.

I can be found at https://mimilaurencewrites.wixsite.com/words
https://www.instagram.com/mimilaurencewrites/
My email address is mimilaurencewrites (at) gmail.com

DON'T FORGET TO LEAVE YOUR REVIEWS

Subscribe to Our Email List

For all romance titles, visit me
Be sure to subscribe to our email list to get new titles "hot off the presses," as well as discount, deals and heads up on new releases.

Sincerely, Mimi Laurence (mimilaurencewrites@gmail.com)

ABOUT THE AUTHOR
Mimi Laurence

Mimi Laurence writes what she sees - hardworking neighbourly people who leave the bad boys and drama queens to others. These ideal friends from all walks of life are the heroes and heroines in Mimi's clean & wholesome and healthy romances. Not Invited to the Wedding is Mimi's first novel, inspired by the great Betty Neels.

An avid reader and traveller, she makes her living advising people how to improve their lives. In Mimi's books, they actually follow her advice!

Her closet contains no athletic shoes nor denim because the best stories only flow when Mimi wears a colourful scarf, one-inch heels, and a jaunty hat.

https://mimilaurencewrites.wixsite.com/words

WRITINGS BY MIMI LAURENCE

Not Invited to the Wedding

After the loss of her grandfather, father, and brother, Katharine was left

grappling with a huge stack of bills. Not being invited to the wedding of the year hardly mattered as the young nurse took the overtime possible.

One blustery morning after a long night at the hospital, she came to the aid of a starving half-blind kitten. Seeing her awesomeness in action, the lonely professor decides his nurse friend is more suited to be his beloved bride. How can Marc get Katharine's attention long enough for her to agree to a white wedding of her very own?

Also available in English audio book format

Available in Spanish as No Fue Invitada a la boda and to Audio book listeners.

Available in French as Elle n'est pas invitee au mariage

Selecting Wine for the Wedding

All of Toronto was agog with the latest gossip: She kicked him out!

Charles had never stopped talking about his wish to leave his job in the family business. Finally, Liz had heard enough of his hare-brained dreams and schemes. He can move in with his parents!

Not even a week later, everyone reports that Charles is seen in the company of someone new. She is by his side at all sorts of galas, concerts, museum events, and more. He has wined and dined her in the best restaurants all over town.

Is Charles trying to make Liz jealous? Or is he really moving on with Elizabeth, a mysterious stranger? Who will be the bride toasted at the wedding?

The Doctor Wants A Wedding

LOST! The little girl had just run around the corner to pet a kitten and now her Nanny has disappeared! All at once, the historical city of Wuxi turned frightening and, with tears streaming down her face, she cried out for her Mummy. Alas, in her native language, Frisian...

Just when all hope seemed lost, a saving angel appeared and took the frightened poppet into her arms, whispering comforting words, the only one in this bustling city to understand the diplomat's daughter.

FOUND! Aletta had her hands full, not just with assignments to grade, but a distraught toddler to reunite with her family. Femke's grateful parents soon insisted on Aletta celebrating Christmas with them in the Netherlands. They even prevailed upon their cousin, the distinguished physician, Baron Friso Thoe van der Veer, to escort her during the festivities and back to Canada.

NOW that he has found the woman of his dreams, the doctor sees a wedding in the future. But how can Friso conduct his courtship of Aletta with the entire width of the Atlantic Ocean in the way?

Tango to the Wedding

CHANGE PARTNERS? Audrey did not have much free time so it was important to enjoy her weekly dance lessons. However there was scant delight on the dance floor since breaking off her engagement... to her tango partner! Now with the Victoria tango dance festival coming up, she found herself faced with a choice, to let her ex take the lead role or take a chance on a new member at the club, Constantine.

The best man at Vancouver Island's tango competition shall be Audrey's partner, at their wedding!

ABOUT THE PUBLISHER

JANICE SETO

Janice Seto writes non-fiction and commentary including articles for The Bridge, the publication of The Malaysia-Canada Business Council. *Save Your Breath: Making Better Deals by Talking Less* is an expansion on her article, on negotiating, for The Bridge. She also has published two books in the JKC Travel Guide series, Ireland 2019 and Argentina 2019.

Over the years, she has studied royalty and studied the Enneagram personality system and written her dissertation on the topic. Royalty Meets Enneagram so far has Royalty Meets Enneagram: Understanding Personality Style 7 Meghan Markle, Sarah Ferguson, Princess Tessy of Luxembourg.

Her more recent books are also available on Amazon: *Standing Out in The Background – A Guide to Extra Work in Toronto's Film & TV Industry* and *Johnny Seto's Bowmanville – An Enneagram Perspective*.

Her first children's book, *Walking for Clean Water: Pukatawagan on the Move*, is in English and Cree, with Ralph Caribou providing the Cree translation.

The System for Women is her first book series on relationships, based on the hilarious but insightful work of Doc Love http://www.doclove.com/. Parts 1 and 3 reached #2 on the Amazon Bestseller list in its category as a free download. Part 5: Pride and Prejudice, JKCs Ireland 2019 travel book and *Bowmanville's Octagon House – From Church and Faith and Tait to Irwin & Seto* also went all the way to #1.

http://janiceseto.wix.com/words
amazon.com/author/janiceseto
www.janiceseto.com

www.ingramcontent.com/pod-product-compliance
Lightning Source LLC
Chambersburg PA
CBHW030557130626
46552CB00006B/2578